what happens in venice

EM SOLSTICE

Copyright © 2025 by Em Solstice

All rights reserved. No part of this publication may be reproduced, stored or transmitted in any form or by any means, electronic, mechanical, photocopying, recording, scanning, or otherwise without written permission from the publisher. It is illegal to copy this book, post it to a website, or distribute it by any other means without permission.

This novel is entirely a work of fiction. The names, characters and incidents portrayed in it are the work of the author's imagination. Any resemblance to actual persons, living or dead, events or localities is entirely coincidental.

First edition

ISBN 9798310477179

To the girls that were loyal but never received loyalty in return. You deserve better.

prologue

"Esme, get off," Rob complained.

I unwrapped my arms from around him. There it was: the constant grumpy whiplash I adored. Physical affection had never been his thing but it *was* mine and I knew he tried, even if, most of the time, he couldn't stand it.

I didn't want to say anything, the argument didn't seem worth it, as he carried on playing his game of

COD on my playstation. Then, on the other hand, I didn't want to show up ridiculously late; we were never on time and it always stressed me out.

"We need to get going soon," I said to him, standing up and walking over to my drawers in the corner of my studio flat. Just *mine*. Because, apparently, it was 'too soon' to move in together. Even after four years. For someone who didn't want to live together, he was there an awful lot of the time.

I pulled my clothes out: a nice black low-cut dress, with a pair of tights to protect me from the winter cold. Black was slinky and it drew attention to the areas of my body that I knew Rob liked the most. Though, as I got changed, he didn't even pay attention, even when I was standing there in my matching green bra and pants.

All I could hear was the sound of shooting; it was starting to give me a headache and I glared at the damn thing. I swear, it was like he was in a relationship with his stupid Call of Duty game, rather than me, which is exactly why I pulled out the black dress in the first place.

I threw my dirty clothes into the washing basket, placed not far from the TV, making sure he would have seen it in the corner of his eye.

It finally gained Rob's attention, his eyes flickering between me and the screen which turned red, indicating he'd died in the game and respawned.

"Fuck's sake," he grumbled.

I rolled my eyes. "Rob, come on. We need to leave in fifteen minutes and you're still playing." I stood next to him, placing my hands on my hips in an attempt to get him to stop gaming and finally get changed.

"Yeah, yeah," he muttered but he started a new round, *still* carrying on shooting people.

"Baby, come on." I reached out to play with his hair, only for him to move his head away from me.

Seconds later, a text came through. That gained his attention for another ten minutes. I wanted to know who was messaging him but Rob kept his screen turned away from me.

When he finally put his phone down to go shower, I peeked. I know I shouldn't have. I never wanted to be that type of girlfriend but I was curious as to who exactly managed to get him off the Playstation, rather than me.

Aimee Work

I recognised the name from conversations we'd had. It made me uncomfortable but what was the point of some useless argument over a text?

By the time Rob was done getting ready, we were twenty minutes late for our dinner with Laura and Liam at the Indian restaurant in town. We were going to celebrate Laura's 25th birthday.

On the rare occasions the four of us would go out together, I was living the dream of the double dates that Laura and I always spoke about growing up. We would plot that it would make our boyfriends the best of friends too and then, as a result, make us a tight knit group. It hadn't happened yet, not in the way we wanted. Rob and Liam made small talk but they were two polar opposites with barely anything in common.

For the entire ride to the restaurant, Rob was on his phone. Just like before, I attempted to look at his screen a few times, finally getting a glance at the name.

Aimee Work

I tightened my knuckles around my steering wheel. The rest of the way to the restaurant, I spent my time trying not to throw up in my mouth.

As I pulled into the car park, he slipped his phone into his pocket, awkwardly shuffling in his seat, with guilt written all over his face.

I walked in, flustered from rushing from the parking spot to the restaurant and trying to push my nausea to the back of my mind. One of the waiters approached us immediately as I spotted Laura and Liam in the corner, sipping on wine. My best friend laughed, dressed in her best little black dress with straightened brown hair down her back.

"Hello, do you have a reservation?" the waiter asked me.

"Yes, thank you. We're booked under my friend, Laura. I can see her over in the corner," I replied.

"Enjoy your meal." The waiter nodded and I walked him towards Laura, with Rob following closely behind, unbothered as usual.

Liam was the one to spot us first, smiling as we reached the table.

"Hey, guys. Sorry we're late. *Someone* was too busy playing COD," I teased, taking a seat next to Laura and handing her a small gift bag, along with a kiss on the cheek.

"We're not *that* late," Rob grumbled, sitting down opposite me.

"I don't know, mate, we've made it through a whole portion of poppadoms while we were waiting." Liam's joking around fell flat with Rob and he shrugged, picking up his menu.

"It's fine, don't worry," Laura dismissed.

"Anyway, happy birthday." I grinned proudly at her as she opened the bag.

We'd never been the type of people to spend loads on one another for birthdays but Laura's tastes were getting more and more boujee as she got older. So, as she was one of my best friends, I pushed the boat out and bought her a Micheal Kors card wallet which cost triple our usual budget.

"Girly, you did not!" she squealed and awkwardly wrapped her arms around me from the side.

"It was on sale but it was so you. I couldn't not get it."

"I love it, thank you." She held it close to her chest.

"Okay, let's eat." Liam rubbed his hands together, then picked up his menu.

"Yes, god please, can we order? I am so hungry."

Then, Rob had to go and open his mouth.

"When aren't you?"

I glared at him, before returning to the menu. I bit my tongue, trying to maintain a nice evening.

Which is exactly the excuse I gave him every time because I loved him.

"Okay, so, while we were waiting, Liam and I were looking at that trip to Venice. We found a decent price for a hotel by the Rialto bridge," Laura spoke up. "I mean, it's nothing special. There are fancier options but Liam said it's in a good place." Her eyes rolled and I laughed at her. After all, my best friend did like the finer things in life now.

"That sounds good," I replied. "I'm so excited. I haven't been on holiday since our trip to Spain that year. And we finally get to go on a gondola." I turned to speak to Rob but his eyes focused on the menu. "Rob?"

"What?" he grumbled, looking at me.

"Venice? Liam and Laura found a hotel."

"Hmm. Great."

"Yeah. Great." I sighed.

Why did I even bother?

six months later

chapter one

I picked up the tea towel and dried off my hands, spinning around to look at my work of art. It was still uncooked but I was proud of myself. The lasagne was a recipe from a handwritten cookbook that my nan had made from the time she was newly married until she was a grandmother. Mom had taken the time to type everything up when Nan had died and had kept the original notebook under wraps on her bookshelf. It was the perfect pick me up to put a smile on Rob's face after work had laid him off.

I packed the bottles of wine in one bag and the wrapped lasagne dish in another, carefully to avoid ruining the presentation. Everything had to be flawless.

I left my tiny studio flat and headed downstairs, trying not to drop anything. Especially my masterpiece of a meal.

Delicately, I placed the dish on the passenger's seat of my Fiat 500 and the bottles of wine in the footwell.

Despite living in the same town, it took longer to get to Rob's house than I liked. We lived on completely different sides but you wouldn't think that a few miles would mean it would take almost half an hour.

Pulling up outside of the house, I parked where Rob's mom usually did. She had left me a spare key underneath one of her plant pots by the front door so I could let myself in.

I felt like an evil genius, managing to sneak into his house and surprise him with dinner. I only hoped that he loved it as much as I wanted him to. Sometimes, his reactions weren't what I expected but it only made me want to try and make him smile even more.

While humming *She Moves in Her Own Way*, I preheated the oven and set up the table by the french doors that led to the garden. By the time dinner was done, the sun would be setting, giving us the perfect backdrop for a romantic meal.

I stood in front of the doors and smiled to myself.

"I'm just that good." I spoke smugly to myself, going to cook the lasagne.

As soon as I shut the door to the oven, I heard a noise coming from upstairs and frowned to myself. No one was meant to be home; Rob was out with his friends and his mom was doing a night shift at the hospital.

Scared, I walked down the hallway and latched onto the bottom post of the stairs. My stomach flipped at a thousand miles an hour.

It could be the end of my life.

Some murderer waiting upstairs to kill me and take the lasagna along with him.

"Hello?" I called up but there was no answer. So, I made the stupid decision to quietly walk up, without even a weapon to protect myself from the supposed intruder.

I climbed the stairs slowly, knowing where the creaks I avoided them. Rustling was coming from one of the rooms but I couldn't quite tell which one it was from.

When I stood at the top of the stairs, I looked around at the doors; they were all shut. There could have been an axe murderer behind any one of them but something made me reach for Rob's room first.

And I wish I never had.

He didn't hear me coming and he didn't notice I was standing in the doorway as he put his clothes back on. There she was too: a mysterious brunette in his bed, with long luscious curls.

Aimee from work.

The girl that'd had me looking over my shoulder every day for the past six months.

Rob turned and we locked eyes. Enough time for his brain to think of some excuse.

"Esme-"

"The lasagne is in the oven." My voice cracked and I spun around on my heel. I had never moved so fast in my entire life. It took me seconds to run down the stairs, grab my phone and keys from the kitchen and slam the door behind me.

It was only when I was outside that I managed to breathe. I climbed into my car, my hands shaking as I put the key into the ignition.

chapter two

I only managed to drive to the end of the street, just around the corner, so he wouldn't be able to see me. Though, I doubted he was even coming after me.

Why would he? When he had his dream girl laying in his bed, waiting to open her legs.

I parked the car at the side of the road and allowed myself to sob, my knuckles wrapping around the steering wheel with so much pressure that they turned white.

I started to question everything I had ever done, trying to find something that I had said that made me deserve my whole world to fall apart. To have the person I love most betray me with some other girl in the bed that I'd slept in countless times. The bed I'd literally helped to build.

My stomach churned.

I *didn't* deserve it.

I chewed on my lip.

I *couldn't* deserve it; I'd done everything that he asked, helped in every way that I could, supported him in everything he wanted in life.

It made sense now, though: all those times he would brush me off, the fact he didn't want to move in and I ended up in a studio flat, all on my own. The more I thought about it, the heavier my crying became.

Once my throat was hoarse and my makeup ruined, I screamed, smashing my hand against the wheel and knocking my car horn. I looked down at my phone in the console, it hadn't even rang yet; he hadn't even cared enough to stop me from leaving.

He didn't chase me, run after me. There hadn't been a sign of remorse or even panic in his eyes.

I wiped away my mascara, took a deep breath to stop my fast-beating heart and drove to the only place I knew I wanted to go. Not a lot of people would consider where they work as the same place to find comfort but, when your best friend worked behind the bar, that's exactly how you felt.

My hands were shaking the entire drive, my bottom lip trembling as I forced myself to keep calm and not end up in an accident. My breathing was uneven, unsteady; it was almost too hard to keep myself together. The saving grace? That his house was only minutes away from the country club that Zoe and I worked at.

I pulled into the staff car park wonky and didn't bother to fix it; that was the last thing on my mind. I took a glance at my phone: still no notifications. He could go fuck himself.

I got out of the car and kept my head down as I made a beeline straight for the bar. Only then, I came to the realisation that the regulars would see me as a snotty mess. Taking a U-turn, I headed back to the car to find my hoodie in the back seat. At least that way I could attempt to hide the state of me.

Pushing open the doors of the lounge, I excused myself as some of the golfers passed me by, heading for the luscious bar on the other side of the large room. The recent renovations had taken it from the old school Peaky Blinders vibes to a sleek, modern approach with lighting that made your eyes hurt, just like the brightness of my friend's blue hair behind the bar.

My lips twitched into a smile as I saw her pop two umbrellas into glasses that were neat whiskey which put a grin on the faces of two of our regulars. Jim and Daniel had been members of the county club since they were in their twenties and, although their arthritis stopped them from golfing, they still came along every couple of days.

I headed for the side of the bar where Zoe went and check her phone now and again during her shift under the guise of chopping fresh lemon and lime.

Slipping onto the stool, I waved my hand to get her attention as she turned to put the expensive whiskey back on the top shelf, using her tippy toes. She caught a glimpse of me and it didn't take long for her demeanor to go from puppy dog to growling rottweiler. Walking over, she placed her arms on the bar, looking like she was going to kill someone.

"What happened?" she asked.

"I... I... he..." I swallowed, trying to find the words to summarise exactly what I had seen. "Rob, he... he was in bed."

"Right?" Zoe nodded slowly, looking over her shoulder to see if anyone needed serving.

"With someone else," I mumbled.

"Say that again?"

"He was in bed with someone else." I looked up and locked eyes with her.

"Oh, you have got to be fucking kidding me," Zoe growled, her hand gripping around her chopping knife, and I was worried she was going to walk out to go murder him right then and there. Instead, she took a deep breath, dropped the knife and reached for her phone. "Okay, so I'm going to text Laura to come and sit with you and then, when I'm on break, we can talk properly. Just stay there okay, babe?"

I nodded and she quickly shot off a text to Laura.

"Do you want a drink?" she asked.

"Vodka," I answered. I didn't need to say anymore than that as the bright, blue-haired beauty poured me a double vodka cranberry without even putting it through the till.

I nursed it, not necking the whole thing like I thought I would have, and stared into space while Zoe served some of the guests. Lifting my hand, I wiped away the tear stains so that I didn't stick out like a sore thumb. My hands were still shaking slightly from the shock coursing through my body. But the adrenaline was beginning to pass and the ache in my chest was louder than the sound of my heart beating in my ears.

Years of my life had been wasted on that good for nothing piece of shit.

There was a tap on my shoulder; it made my blood run cold, until I realised that it was Laura. Her eyes were screaming pity.

I attempted a smile only for my lip to tremble and I broke down into silent sobs.

Laura wrapped her arms around me, holding me against her chest.

"It's okay, Es. I got you," she whispered into my hair.

I nodded and tried to pull back on my crying after lasting twenty minutes without any.

Pulling away, I cleaned under my eyes again as she took a seat next to me. Zoe passed us by and put an orange juice in front of Laura, before having to scurry away to the next customer. The girl acted as if she was on roller skates, gliding around the bar on her own.

"What happened?" Laura asked, taking a sip of her drink.

"I went to Rob's to cook us dinner. Cheer him up after what had happened after work. And I was literally setting a fucking romantic table for dinner. But I heard something upstairs. So, I went up and there he was, getting dressed while some slag was lying in his bed." The adrenaline was swapped out for anger now.

"Woah. What a prick. Did you see who it was?"

I shook my head. "She was turned away, looked like she was sleeping or some shit. He hasn't even tried to call me or at least he didn't while I was driving. But he didn't chase after me either. All I've ever done is worship the ground he walks on and I do everything I can to support him. And that's what I get in return?"

My eyes started to water again as I turned away to take a deep breath and get myself under control.

"He doesn't deserve you." Laura rubbed my back.

That's when Zoe walked over to us and leaned on the lower counter, fury still plastered on her face.

"Wait til I get my hands on him," Zoe snarked.

"He doesn't care so I don't care," I sniffed. It was a complete and utter lie to both them and myself.

"It's going to take time for you to be okay." Zoe reached out and took my hand.

I offered a sad smile and a small nod.

"You can do so much better," Laura added. Then, before she could open her mouth again, her phone rang. She turned it over so she could see who it was. "That's my mom wondering where I am. I said I'd go round for dinner." She looked at me. Pity. Her eyes were filled with pity. And I hated it. "Are you going to be okay?"

"Yeah, I'm going to finish this." I lifted my drink. "And then head home. I think I need a little alone time to think everything through."

"I'll text you when I can." Laura slipped off the stool and pressed a kiss to my teary cheek.

"Okay, love you."

"Love you too! See you later, Zo. Thanks for the drink."

"Anytime."

chapter three

Once Laura had left, Zoe managed to have her twenty minute break. I sobbed in the staffroom while other team members banged on the door, telling Zoe to open up. But, there were some perks of being the shift leader.

I dumped my snotty tissue in the bin in the corner of the room and turned to Zoe.

"I'm going to head home," I told her.

"You're not driving." She folded her arms, raising her brow. My friend's protective instincts were coming out; that or she didn't want to walk home tonight.

"I'm going to catch the bus, don't worry. Let me get my phone out of the car and then I'll come give you my keys; you can drive it back to yours later."

"Are you sure?"

"Positive." I faked a smile. That was no way believable but Zoe accepted my effort.

After handing my keys over to her, I gave her a small wave while she was sorting out one of the regulars and dipped out. The sun had set now and the chill was setting in; I wrapped my jacket around myself as I headed towards the bus stop which was sat by a pub and a chippy. Luckily, the country club wasn't too far from civilisation.

I had a while until the bus came to take me back to my cold and lonely flat... at least it all made sense now why Rob never wanted to move in with me; he wouldn't have been able to fuck his mistress if I was home.

I walked into the fluorescent-lit chippy, owned by a lovely elderly couple whose son owned the pub next door. There was no one waiting to be served and the wife was quietly organising the drinks fridge.

"Hello?" I called out and she turned to me with a big smile.

"Hello, dear. What can I get you?"

"Could I have a cone of chips with curry sauce please?" I said, pulling my card out the back of my phone case.

"Make that two please, Gloria. I got this."

Standing behind me was Liam, Laura's boyfriend, his shaggy brown curls drooping over his eyes. He looked like he was dressed for a night out with his mates. I glanced at my phone; it was barely nine. So, why was he in the chippy and heading home so early on in the night?

"Thanks," I said. "How come you're here, bored of the pub already?"

"Didn't fancy it. Why are you in this neck of the woods?"

"Rob and I broke up," I answered simply and turned away from him. Gloria took a glance over from scooping chips into the first tray.

"Oh, right," Liam replied softly. He shuffled awkwardly on his feet, looking anywhere other than at me.

I shrugged my shoulders, feeling the numbness setting into my core. Gloria handed me the first chips with sauce and I thanked her, then Liam.

As I walked out of the door, Liam called, "Wait up, Esme." He quickly dumped Gloria a bunch of change with his chips in hand and walked towards me. "Let me sit with you, just while you wait for the bus?"

"Sure." Liam had always been kind to me, almost like we were siblings, just because of him and Laura. They had been dating for over seven years, straight out of sixth form and thrown into the real world.

Liam dropped into step beside me as we strolled towards the bus stop in silence. Once there, I perched myself on the uncomfortable and narrow bench, finding myself staring out across the road. The numbness was starting to settle in and I was disassociating from the events of the day, my whole life falling apart.

"So, what happened?" Liam asked, using one of the small, wooden forks for his chips.

"Oh, shit; I forgot a fork." I sighed.

Liam reached into his pocket and pulled out another, handing it to me.

"Oh, thanks. He... well, he cheated on me; I saw him in bed with some girl. I don't know who, though."

"I'm sorry," he spoke sincerely but it took me a second to know what to say.

"He hasn't even called, so what's the point of caring?" I nibbled a bit off one of my chips, coming to the realisation that I wasn't even that hungry after all that.

"You deserve better. We both do."

I flicked my head towards him.

"What do you mean?" I raised a brow, about to go into fight mode for my best friend's honor. She was my best friend; it's what best friends did, took one another's side.

"She didn't tell you, did she?" He rolled his eyes and stared off to the empty field opposite us. "Laura and I broke up last week."

"You did?" It was the first that I had heard of it and I questioned why she hadn't been the one to tell me.

Liam nodded, swallowing the food in his mouth.

"Um, why?" I asked, completely forgetting that my own life had exploded only a few hours ago. Mine could wait, though; my friends came first and I wanted to make sure I didn't need to go look after her.

"We had a big argument about moving forward with our lives and it didn't end well; she didn't want to move in. It was a whole thing."

Something told me there was more to the story but the look on Liam's face told me that he didn't want to talk about it anymore. I bet if I were to look into the mirror then, my eyes would tell the same story about my own relationship issues.

"I'm still planning to go on that trip to Venice next week."

Another thing that I had forgotten about. The double date holiday to Venice that the four of us had booked. I guessed that it was in the water, just like the city would be in a few centuries.

"I haven't taken anyone's name off the booking yet. I mean, it's not like either of them paid towards it anyway. You know, just in case you wanted to come? Maybe it would be good for you to get away as well."

"Hmm?" I asked.

"Come with me, Esme. I changed it to a twin room. We could go as friends; I mean, if you wanted to."

Escape to Europe with my best friend's ex because my own love life was in tatters?

I looked over at the field, considering it. I was already half packed with holiday booked off at work; there was nothing stopping me. Besides, I liked Liam; I considered him a friend, one that I didn't want to lose just because he and Laura weren't together anymore.

"Okay." I nodded. "Let's go to Venice."

chapter four

T-minus one day to go.

I was almost packed and only needed to grab some of those tiny toiletries from Boots. That's all I wanted to do as well but, instead, I was being dragged around every single shop in Birmingham town centre, each level of the Bullring. My feet hurt and I didn't want to do any more shopping. Which is why I was thankful that my mom finally wanted to sit down and have a coffee break.

I collapsed into the chair, dropping her bags that I had been forced to carry.

"What are you complaining about? You love shopping." Mom laughed.

"I'm going to have enough walking around over the next few days. I only needed some shampoo and conditioner."

"Aww, poor baby," she cooed, leaning over to pinch my cheek.

"Mom," I whined and moved away.

My mom was never afraid to embarrass me. She was a hard worker and had been through a lot but she never let it get her down. She was always dressed to impress and, while her makeup skills weren't flawless, she was well presented with a short cropped hairstyle.

"What would you like, baby?" She stood to head over to the counter.

"Hot chocolate, please."

She ruffled my hair as she passed and I tutted, flattening my hair back down.

While my mom was ordering, I pulled out my phone to check my messages. There were a few missed calls from Rob, which made my stomach drop, and then there was a message notification from Liam.

Avoiding Rob was becoming a new habit.

And I wasn't sure how to feel about that yet.

But I turned my attention back to the other option, opening the message to find a YouTube link that led me to a video called 'Cat vs. Printer'. It didn't take long for it to make me laugh.

He'd been doing it all week, sending me videos that would cheer me up, ready for our trip to Venice. I appreciated it because, without those moments, I would have still been wallowing in bed, watching time pass me by.

Mom came back with a tray, two hot chocolates, a croissant and a blueberry muffin, placing them down on our table like a little feast.

"What's got you smiling?" She raised her brow, on to me as she sat down again.

"Nothing, just some video that Zoe sent me," I lied. "Thank you for this."

"I'm proud of you, you know that? Last year you would have never even considered going on holiday on your own."

I hated lying to her but going on holiday with your best friend's ex wasn't going to get me a daughter of the year award. The guilt was eating me alive, though. I wished I could have spoken to her about it all because I really didn't know what the hell I was doing by agreeing to do this trip.

"Yeah, the peace and quiet will do me the world of good," is what I settled for.

"How are you feeling?"

"I'm okay."

"Don't lie to me. I'm your mother."

I chuckled at her. "I'm okay, I'm getting there. I deserve better, I know I do. I'm starting to look back on our relationship... it hadn't been good for a while. So, it was for the best." It was hard to speak about because everything was still piecing itself together in my head; I just knew that there had to be something better out there for me. *Someone* better.

"I'm just proud of you. I wanted to tell you that he wasn't right for you but, as a mother who didn't listen to her own, I knew that you needed to realise for yourself. I'm here for you, okay, darling?" Mom reached out and took my hand, stroking the back of it. Her skin was soft against mine, soothing me like she used to do when I was little. Even after everything I'd done, the mistakes I'd made, she'd always been there for me, in her own way, making sure I'm okay.

And that's why I began to hold back my tears as I squeezed back, all my emotions spilling out.

"I know, thank you. Anyway, happier things. How's the book club?"

Which only led Mom to an in-depth ramble about the latest smutty book they were reading. I wish I never asked because who wants to know their mom's kinky fantasies?

chapter five

How on earth had I ended up in Birmingham airport waiting for my best friend's ex? With my tiny, orange cabin suitcase and handbag, ready for five days in the Italian summer heat? Yet there I was, waiting upstairs, near the entrance of fast lane security, for Liam, who was already twenty minutes later than he said he would be.

I was on edge, as if I expected Laura to pop out at me at any second and call out 'busted' for running away with her ex boyfriend.

I hadn't told her. I wasn't quite sure why I had kept it a secret but even Liam agreed to keep it between us that we were still heading on the romantic couple's trip the four of us had booked together. It had been on my mind, though, that she hadn't told me and something was obviously going on with her. And, I had barely seen her over the past week, just like I had barely spoken to Rob.

He had finally texted the morning after I'd caught him cheating, a small 'hey' which had set off a flurry of anger inside of me. I'd called him, not that he had answered, and then lobbed my phone so hard across the room that it cracked and I could barely see my screen anymore. My heart was shattered along with it because of the confusion he had sent coursing through my body.

It wasn't until hours later that he called me back, with no real answer as to why he'd done what he had, why he had taken everything that I had done for him and thrown it all away.

I sighed, checking my cracked screen, then looked over at the escalator. Thankfully, Liam was stepping off it and heading for me, with his bag over his shoulder, dressed in some swanky shirt and shorts.

"You're late," I told him the moment he was close enough to hear me.

"My taxi was caught in traffic. We still have two and half hours, don't worry." He smiled like a cheeky schoolboy, as if that would calm me down. "Did something happen?"

"No. Nothing happened," I said. "But I haven't told Laura where I'm going and I am beginning to feel like the biggest piece of shit there is." I sighed, brushing my hair in shame that I was keeping secrets.

"Hey, coming on this trip is meant to cheer us both up and we're not doing anything wrong. But, if you feel *that* bad, we don't have to go. You can always head home."

I took a glance at the security arch, allowing myself a moment to think about it, before shaking my head.

"No, let's go." I deserved the break. I'd had a week from hell and barely made it through my shifts at work without crying.

"Let's do this, then. We're gonna have a great time." Liam attempted to be cheery but even I could see the lack of happiness in his eyes. He was struggling as much as I was and I didn't quite know why they'd broken up, other than 'We just fell out of love' because that's all he would tell me.

I decided not to push any further on it, not until Liam was ready to talk. Instead, I concentrated on getting myself onto the plane and the piece of freedom that awaited me.

And nothing could ever compare to the feeling of walking through security and lining up with all the other people ready to get out of stormy England. The queue was short, surprisingly, even for fast track, and it wasn't long until it was our turn to take our electronics out of our bags and step under the detector. I went through without a problem and waited with my things on the other side.

Liam, on the other hand, *had* been stopped; the security workers rummaged through his bag that had way more pockets than it needed.

"It's just a face mask," he told them as they held up a green clay mask tub.

I laughed quietly to myself; I hadn't known that Liam was so into his skin care.

"Why is it green?" the guy asked, suspicious, as though it was going to be anything else other than a mix of avocado or something.

"Because it's good for your skin. Keep it if you need to; maybe you can take it home and try it for yourself." Liam plastered a smile on his face with his backhanded comment.

The security worker raised his eyebrow at him and swiped the pot of face mask under the counter, before zipping up his bag and handing it over to him.

"Thanks, mate, enjoy." He nodded and walked towards me.

"You could have gotten yourself kicked off the flight."

"Nah, I'm too charming for that." Liam winked; he was far too proud for my liking.

"Come on, we have time to kill before our gate opens and I need a glass of wine." I grabbed the handle of my suitcase and dragged it down the corridor to the duty free area, where Wetherspoons was calling my name.

It was hard to resist all of the luxury makeup and alcohol that was sitting tax free and begging me to buy it. We were passing the Swarovski stand as we were exiting the duty free shop and I stopped in my tracks, looking at the shining jewellery under the harsh lighting. My fingers fumbled over the various boxes they were displayed in until I picked one up. The square box was home to a small, delicate tennis bracelet with baby blue crystals. A travel exclusive and absolutely beautiful. I checked the back of the box for the price, then put it back down, telling myself I had more than enough bracelets and definitely didn't need another.

Liam was standing not too far away from me; he had wandered over to the whiskey section only a metre or so away. I thought back to when he and Laura started dating and she had shown me a picture of his back at the gym, the rippling muscle kind, and you could see it all under his shirt. Then, my admiration turned to guilt as I reminded myself that I was running away to another country with her ex and hadn't told her.

"Hey, you ready?" I called out. There was no turning back so I just had to carry on making the decision that could potentially ruin my oldest friendship.

Liam looked over his shoulder. "I'll meet you at Spoons; I'm just gonna grab a bottle of something."

"Okay, no problem," I replied and turned around to head into the main area of the airport. The Wetherspoons wasn't far from where we were and I managed to find a two person table on the edge of the open area. Despite being in the middle of the airport, it still managed to have its dark, wooden textures across the bar and seating area. The floor was still slightly sticky and the tables weren't exactly the cleanest but what else would you expect from 'Spoons', the Great British staple?

I picked my phone out of my handbag and pulled up the camera to scan the QR code, ordering myself a large glass of Villa Maria wine. Pulling up the ciders, knowing that Liam preferred those from when we had been on double dates. I added a strawberry and lime cider to my order as well. Once I'd paid for the drinks, then pulled up Instagram, I scrolled aimlessly to kill it time.

A couple of minutes later, a young man approached the table with a tray and placed down both drinks in front of me.

"Thank you," I said to him, offering a small smile.

"Enjoy," he replied and the server walked away, leaving me alone.

I picked up the glass and let the cold wine touch my lips and calm me down. It didn't last long, though, as a WhatsApp message from Laura popped up on my phone, wishing me a safe trip. All she knew was that I'd got a last minute deal and was heading out on my own. The guilt swallowed me again as Liam sat down opposite me, with a duty free bag that he placed on the table.

"Hey, I got you a cider." I pushed the bottle towards him.

"Great, cheers. I'm parched."

"So, I think we need a few rules for this trip."

"Okay, sure." Liam shrugged and leaned back in his chair.

It was funny how, once you were single, you started to see people in a different light. There was no denying Liam was good looking and I couldn't help myself that I stared one second longer than I should have at his muscular arms.

Which I should definitely not have.

"Right, I think the main one is that no one gets changed in the room; we use the bathroom. And I need to shower first because I have to do my hair and makeup. Also, no pictures together; we can't have any trace that we were on this trip together."

"Agreed."

"Okay, good."

Turns out, the more wine I drank, the better I felt about the trip; my 'wine goggles' were firmly on. The time passed quickly; we exchanged stories of our customers, the funny and scary ones. Liam was a chef in a pub in town and he eventually wanted to open his own. He had talked about his dream since I had met him a couple of years ago and credit to him because he had been working up the hierarchy since.

Once our gate was open, we headed straight for it, hoping to not be in the back of the queue to get on. Liam passed me my boarding pass for the way there and back while we were waiting. So far, everything was fine, until we reached the front to get our passes checked. The air host scanned our tickets with a plastered smile on her face. She looked between us as we passed her our passports.

"How adorable." She gushed, placing her hand on her chest. "Is it your anniversary or just a romantic get away?" she asked.

"Oh, no, no; we're just friends." I put my hands up and shook my head.

"Oh my god, I am so sorry." The hostess panicked.

"It's okay," Liam answered. "'City of Romance' and all that; but we're just here for a good time."

"Well, you're all ready to set off," she said, passing us back our passports.

We walked forwards and down the ramp that took us outside, where cones were laid out to create a path leading to the plane. There was something about seeing it for the first time, the bubble of excitement growing in my stomach, and I couldn't help but smile. I finally gave myself the chance to enjoy something and told myself that I deserved it.

But then, the sound of my ringtone echoed in my bag as we got closer to the steps. I pulled it out and my stomach churned at the name of the screen.

Rob calling...

I clicked the reject button and dumped it back in my bag. He was not going to take this away from me too; I'd cried too many tears over him already.

chapter six

There was nothing like stepping onto the plane and knowing that, soon enough, you'd be in the sky. I'd always been okay when it came to taking off and landing but being up in the sky for a long period of time, where anything could happen, terrified me.

"Do you want to sit by the window?" Liam asked.

"Please." Were planes terrifying? Yes. But I still wanted the window seat, just so I could always see what was happening.

He stepped forward to let me into our seats and, before I could even lift my case, Liam took it from me and placed it over my head into the overhead storage with ease.

"Thanks." I smiled.

After sitting down in my seat and putting my handbag in front of me so I could get comfy, I put my seatbelt on. Liam had put his own case above too and then taken the seat next to mine. Our legs were touching... I inched away, trying to press myself against the plane as much as possible. I watched Liam put on his own seatbelt and pull the flight shopping magazine from the netting on the seat in front of us, turning to the random selection of perfumes and watches.

I took my phone out of my bag, glancing at the missed call and one new message that sat on my lock screen.

Heard you're going on holiday. Where are you going?

As if I was going to tell him, as if he had any right to my life anymore. Because he should have been sitting right next to me, not between the legs of some other random girl. I turned my phone on airplane mode and pulled out my AirPods to watch the episodes of *The Vampire Diaries* that I had downloaded; this would easily pass the time and I wouldn't have to hold any conversations with Liam. Though, I knew I would have to at some point if we were about to spend the next few days with each other.

It wasn't long until we were up in the sky and flying towards the sinking island of Venice with the other holiday goers. The hostess from earlier had been right though; the plane was mostly filled with happy couples.

...

I didn't know when I had fallen asleep and I didn't know how I had ended up with my head resting on Liam's shoulder. My arm was hanging over his front, my fingers toying with the hem of his shirt and Liam's head was resting on top of mine. I stayed still, not sure what to do or say in the situation. I must have been the first one to fall asleep based on our positions. I wasn't quite sure why he hadn't moved me as soon as my head had ended up on his shoulder.

To make the matter worse, my ear was hurting from my AirPod being pressed into my ear against him.

I slowly moved my hand, then gently began to pull my head away, only that, of course, moved his too and Liam woke with a startled look on his face.

"Sorry. I didn't mean..."

"No, no, it's okay; you seemed comfy and, well, sorry for falling asleep on you." A surprise blush swept across Liam's cheeks.

I shook my head. "It's fine, guess we're as bad as each other." I glanced out the window; the sun was setting and I could see the airport below us as the plane swung around for landing. "I think we're about to touch down," I said, yawning.

"Thank fuck; I have this pain in my knee and it's killing me," Liam groaned.

"How old are you?" I joked.

"Twenty-five going on fifty-two," he replied.

Ten minutes later, we were firmly on the floor again and everyone else on the plane shoved and pushed to get off the plane. Liam and I glanced at one another; no way in hell were we joining in on that. Instead, we let most people leave, before grabbing our cases down and going ourselves.

Waiting for us and the rest of the passengers was one of those stuffy mini buses that never actually had enough space to fit everyone on. Although it wasn't hot, it would be on that blasted thing.

"After you?" Liam held out his hand.

I took a step onto the bus, dragging my case with me, trying to find somewhere I could hold on. Liam tried to put as much space between us as he could, only for us to be pushed closer together when more passengers stepped on. We were almost touching. I cleared my throat and looked away, avoiding eye contact.

When everyone was crammed on, the bus began to move, rattling along the runway to take us to the main airport.

I wasn't expecting the sharp corner it took, I didn't even know that it *could* turn like that. When it did, though, there was no stopping my body slamming right into Liam. I gasped as his reflexes reached for my hip to stop me from falling over.

I looked up and swallowed.

"Sorry."

"It's fine, it's not your fault these things are death traps."

I repositioned myself and pulled away from him, his hand dropping from my waist.

"Yeah, I'd rather bloody walk," I muttered. That way, it would save me from being touched by my best friend's ex.

I was thankful when the bus stopped and we got off, regaining my personal space as we walked into arrivals.

Going through passport control was easy enough; it flew by as our plane was the only one that had landed recently. Without the need to grab any bags, we went straight for the transfer. Both of us were looking around at the various people standing about. There, by one of the airport pillars, was 'Mcallister, party of four'.

"I amended the booking; why does it say that?" He huffed and took strides towards our driver. Something bad must have gone down between Laura and him a couple of weeks ago for his mood to change so drastically.

I followed after him and kept quiet as he spoke to our driver, heading towards the car park where a black minivan was waiting for us. It was lined with pretty blue LED lights and opposite us were two empty seats; the wave of missing Rob returned and I had to remind myself as we set off that this break was meant to be about moving on from him.

I had to find myself again. The person I was without him. Because I could barely remember her myself. The longer I was apart from Rob, the more I realised how much of myself I'd lost. I didn't even have fun anymore.

The drive was quiet; neither of us really said a word, our eyes just locked on the seats in front of us. I wanted to say something, I just wasn't sure what. Most of the time we'd spent together was with Laura and Rob, never alone. It seemed stupid to ask about the weather or something else just as pointless. I decided that staying quiet was the best way forward, at least for now.

Fifteen minutes later, we were pulling up into the car park on the edge of Venice, the driver taking our luggage out for us. I climbed out of the car too, Liam following, as we thanked him for bringing us. But it didn't take long for my attention to be pulled elsewhere.

As soon as I saw the dusk sky over the buildings, dancing on the water, all my worries disappeared. It finally hit me that I was in another country and I didn't have to worry or think of anything about back home while I was here. I was beyond excited to see every sight, visit every store and eat every inch of pizza that I could get my hands on. A whole new world to explore and not a single ex in sight, if you didn't count my best friend's.

"You ready?" Liam stood next to me, looking down at his phone for directions, with his duffel bag on his shoulder. "This says we have a fifteen minute walk to the hotel."

"Yeah, let's go. Lead the way."

Liam's strides were much bigger than mine and I struggled to keep up while also admiring my surroundings. The canals were surprisingly not as smelly as people made out. There was the sound of birds above us but there was also a lot more graffiti on the outer edges than I expected; some walls were covered in it completely. Then, as we got further into the main city, we were passing bakeries, gift shops and restaurants. Some of the servers were already trying to pull us in to stuff our faces with pasta and wine. Liam was quick to reply with the bit of Italian that he knew which they seemed to appreciate.

"How long is this going to take?" I called, trying to dodge the tourists getting ready for their dinner.

"We're only a few minutes away." He looked over his shoulder.

In the worst timing possible, the sound of my suitcase dragging across the path rang in my ears and I turned around to find that my wheel was hanging on by a thread.

"Oh, for fuck's sake," I growled.

Liam must have heard me because he turned and stepped back towards me.

"Here, give it to me. I got you." He reached over, collapsing the handle down, before picking it up.

A small smile danced on my lips. "Thank you. What about the directions, though?" I asked.

"It's just round this corner, we'll be fine. Come on, I'm starving."

We walked for another minute and came out on the grand canal by the Rialto bridge, with crowds of tourists taking photos and people having their dinner while watching the gondolas and water taxis. The staple bridge was nothing short of beautiful, with the intricate carved stone and the archway right in the centre that led to a series of small shops on the other side. There was no question as to why it was a tourist destination.

I pulled out my phone, snapping a quick picture, Liam waiting patiently beside me.

"Isn't that stunning?" I said to him.

"Italy will never cease to amaze me. Hotel is just on the other side." He nodded across the canal.

Without my case, I was quicker walking up the steps of the bridge but Liam kept his pace with me, despite carrying both of our things.

"I think I might officially be excited," I squealed, standing at the top of the bridge, looking over at the water. "Can you take a photo of me?" I passed over my phone.

"Yeah, course I can."

Once I'd done the same for him, we descended the steps and towards our hotel.

Hotel Rialto's lobby was large and spacious. The floor was checkered with pieces of cream and burnt orange marble with a big check-in desk. Opposite, there were black leather sofas that threw off the interior design a little but they were still nice. Flowers were placed on the coffee tables and there was warm lighting dotted around the area. It looked like a lobby you would get back home but no, this one was in Venice. It changed the atmosphere; everything became more luxurious thanks to the vintage furnishings and the Italian accents of the staff.

There was nothing that could stop me smiling in that moment.

We approached the desk and an elderly man looked up from his computer with a wide smile.

"Hi," Liam spoke, letting him know that we were English speakers. "We have a room booked under Mcallister for four nights?"

"One moment, sir." He looked down at his computer, typing away. "Yes, here we are. Double room for four nights."

"No, sorry; I emailed ahead and said we needed a twin room. I was told it had been changed?" Liam looked startled.

I knew exactly where this was going and I didn't like the sound of it.

"We're very sorry, sir, but all of our twin rooms have been taken. Double is all that we have."

Liam and I looked at each other. One bed. And no way out of it.

"How do you feel about it?" he asked.

"We'll be fine. We can just put a pillow between us," I joked.

As if it wasn't bad enough that I was on holiday with my best friend's ex.

Now I had to share a bed with him as well.

chapter seven

I couldn't say that I managed to sleep well the entire night. I kept rolling into the pillow wall that we had built between us, even though I positioned myself on the edge of the bed. All I knew was that we had managed not to touch while we slept and that was a good thing.

The room was nice but strange; I'd never seen walls that were padded and covered in fabric. The mint green made it a little more subtle. Our bed had an intricate headboard with hand-painted details and the sheets matched the walls. There was also a desk with the same white with gold painted details. I blinked a few times, trying to adjust to the light.

Catching myself from rolling out of bed, I realised that I was in it alone and sat up to look around the room. Liam was standing at the window, the large wooden shutters wide open like something out of a Disney movie. He was only wearing the shorts he went to bed in, his t-shirt gone. I couldn't not notice the muscles in his back with the way his arms were flexed, leaning out of the window. The struggle to remind myself that he was so far off limits for so many reasons escaped me as I admired him. Only, it left me feeling like a bad person.

How he and Laura ever broke up was lost on me. They were quite literally the perfect couple; she plastered him all over her Instagram. I picked up my phone and searched for her profile. The number of posts was down and, with a quick scroll, I confirmed that every trace of Liam was gone. The question that ran through my mind again, *why hadn't she told me?*

Surely, if Liam had done something, then she would have at least said?

"Morning."

I jumped at the sound of Liam's voice and put down my phone. The last thing I wanted was to get caught stalking his social media and look like a weirdo. "Morning."

"Sleep okay?" he asked, turning around and giving me an eye full of his abs.

"Um, yeah, good," I answered.

"I'm just going to shower and then I was going to talk to reception again, see if any twin rooms were checked out while you got ready. I know you wanted to be the first to shower. But I was hoping I could be quick before you woke up. "

"It's okay, you can shower. I was going to have one later. And yeah, sounds good. So, do you have a plan for what you wanna do today?" I asked.

"I was just thinking, let's find our bearings? Get breakfast? Then, maybe plan some stuff for the next couple of days?"

"Yeah, okay, great."

"Okay, well, I'll just go shower. I won't be long." He picked up a towel and a pile of clothes from the desk, sticking to the 'get dressed in the bathroom' rule.

When I heard the door lock, I got out of bed to open my suitcase. I pulled an outfit for the day, deciding on a white summer dress and my matching trainers as I already felt the sun coming through the open window. I set out my makeup and travel mirror on the desk and started to apply my foundation.

Like Liam, I took a moment to take in the sights from our room window. We'd been lucky enough to get the perfect view of the bridge and the canal. The city was just waking up, restaurants were putting out their tables and chairs, cafe's opening up and gondolas being uncovered and lined up along the water. There wasn't a cloud in the sky. I took a photo, wanting to save the moment forever, and then sat down to start getting ready.

In the middle of my makeup, Liam came out, fully dressed, with his curly hair pulled into a bun; a few strands hadn't made it and were falling down the side of his face. Another moment where I was seeing Liam in a different light than before. He looked good, better than good, with the way his hair was framing his face. I couldn't keep allowing myself to think like that.

"Gonna head down, I'll be back in a minute," he said, grabbing his phone and hotel key card from his side of the bed.

"Okay, I should be done by the time you get back."

Liam was kind but that wasn't news to me; I'd always got that impression. What I *was* surprised about was how considerate he was. Knowing how uncomfortable I was about the bed, he was going to ask again. I got the impression that he wouldn't stop asking until he made it happen either.

It was a human thing to do but I began to realise that normal human things weren't something I was used to. For years, I'd only thought about Rob and he had only thought about himself.

I had a lot to relearn about myself, things to learn to love again for myself, rather than for someone else, just like my enjoyment of makeup. Something I used to look forward to doing every day.

Once I'd applied my setting spray, I dipped into the bathroom to get changed, coming out to see Liam chilling on the bed, looking through his phone.

"Any luck?" I asked.

Liam looked up at me and shook his head. "None at all, wouldn't even offer us a discount for a second room, even though there was another originally on the booking."

"Damn. Well I guess it worked, right? The whole pillow thing?"

"Yeah, I don't mind carrying on with that, if you don't mind, that is?"

"Then that's sorted." I picked up my plain black crossbody bag and hooked it over my shoulder. "It's nine-thirty, wanna head out?"

We didn't wander far; only a few minutes away from our hotel was Piazza San Marco. It was still quiet as we found a small cafe just past the crowd, looking over the water. The sun was beaming down, giving us an opportunity to sit outside and watch the boats. I ordered myself a tea and a croissant while Liam ordered a coffee, telling me he wasn't a breakfast person.

There was comfortable silence between us as we took in the sun and watched people pass us by.

"I'm glad I came," I spoke. "I needed this, I needed to get away."

"I'm glad you did too; I think it would have been boring alone."

"Are you ever going to tell me why you and Laura broke up? Because she hasn't either." I took a sip of my tea, my eyes trained on him, waiting to see if he would open up.

Liam placed down his cup; was he actually going to tell me?

"Not yet, still processing." His lips turned up into a sad smile and I frowned.

"I'm not going to have to kill you, am I? You didn't hurt her?"

"No. Never. I would never have." He shook his head. "I won't expect you to believe me but why would I risk bringing you with me if I'd done something that was going to get me castrated in my sleep? She hurt *me* in the end. I'm just not ready to talk about it." He sounded sincere; there was an edge in his voice that was almost like he was holding back tears. Even though Laura was my friend, it felt wrong to push any further.

"I'll respect that. I know what it's like to be hurt by someone you love. So, when you're ready, you can tell me; it won't go anywhere, just between us."

The twinkle in Liam's eyes came back as he lifted his coffee up. "What happens in Venice, stays in Venice?" He smirked, our glasses clinking together.

"Cheers to that."

chapter eight

My legs felt like they were about to fall off; we'd been walking for hours and got lost down countless alleys. I lay back on the bed, sweat dripping off me and pains creeping up the back of my thighs.

"I think I'm dead," I groaned.

"I'm more dead," Liam mumbled from the desk chair, sipping at his water bottle.

"I don't think I'll ever be able to move again."

"What, even for dinner?"

"I could be tempted by pasta and wine." I sat up and sighed. "But I need a full blown shower; I'm stinking."

"Same here, you go first. I'll just chill, maybe ring my mom."

"I won't be long."

I showered and washed my hair as quickly as I could, then dried my hair slightly so it wouldn't drip all over my clothes. My outfit was a snug pink bandeau dress with a subtle floral print and a slit up one leg which was decorated by a light ruffle; although, it wasn't done any justice by the knotted bleached blonde mess, also known as my hair. I picked up my towel and hairbrush, walking out into the room while starting to brush the knots out.

Liam was in the same spot, holding his phone up.

"Sorry, Mom, I'm going to have to dash; I need to shower and then I'm going out for dinner."

"Okay, sweetie. Have fun and I'll speak to you soon," his mom replied.

"All done?" he asked.

I nodded.

"I'm digging the dress, Es. It suits you. You look amazing."

I couldn't remember the last time I'd been called 'amazing' and that was a sad realisation. "Thank you." I said, blushing. "Well, I should sort this mop out." I pointed to my hair.

Liam stood up, dusting his hands on his jeans. "Yeah, course; I'm gonna, um, go shower." He grabbed his dried towel from the morning and scrambled for some clothes.

While he did that, I dried my hair, finally able to pull it back into a ponytail on the nape of my neck, and then started to reapply makeup. With the sun having set, it meant that it wasn't going to boil off me.

I was working on my eyeliner when Liam came out of the bathroom, dressed already. He walked over to his bag on the other side of the room, pulling out his hairdryer with a diffuser attached. He started to dry his curls as I finished my makeup but I found myself watching him in the mirror. He took care of himself; I liked that about him. I hadn't realised the effort it took for his curls to look like that until I watched him scrunch in gels and oils while using a diffuser on his hair.

I finished my makeup with Morphe setting spray at the same time that Liam finished his hair. But then, my phone started to vibrate beside me, Rob lighting up the screen again, and I felt the urge to throw my phone across the room. I clicked the reject button almost immediately, Liam clocking on straight away.

"I blocked Laura, if that helps. Not that she ever had anything to say unless it was a bitchy remark." Liam sighed. "Sorry again; she's your friend." He sat down on the bed. Whatever was going through his head was stressing him out and I didn't want Liam to have a shitty time because he had to worry about what he could and couldn't say about Laura. He was one of kindest people I'd met and he didn't have anyone; my heart hurt for him.

"Hey, don't worry about it," I told him. "I get what you're going through and we agreed that what happens in Venice, stays in Venice. So, if you need to vent, then vent; I guess I just won't be joining you on the Laura hate train but you're exes. It makes sense." I felt like a complete bitch; what kind of person lets someone talk shit about their best friend, especially when it's their best friend's ex boyfriend? I should have been hating on the man with Laura back home but, then again, I couldn't guarantee that she would have even told me if I hadn't found out.

"Thanks but I should keep it to a minimum. Seriously, you should block him if he's just gonna upset you."

"I'm hoping he is starting to get the picture and leave me alone."

"You deserve better, Esme. I mean that." Liam offered me a sad smile with his kind words and I tried to give one back.

"Shall we go for dinner?" I asked, wanting to change the subject before I cried and had streams of makeup down my cheeks.

...

Surprisingly, dinner with my best friend's ex-boyfriend wasn't as awkward as I had thought it would be; the longer we spent around one another, the more comfortable it was. It felt like we were building some sort of forbidden friendship that we wouldn't be able to tell anyone about. But, it was easier for me to talk about Rob than it was for Liam to talk about Laura. He was probably afraid that I'd tell her everything he said or beat him up for treating my best friend the wrong way.

In a cliche fashion, we had both ordered pizza. I went for one with homemade meatballs and Liam went for chicken and ham.

Only, Liam's face was a picture when his meal was placed in front of him, curling up in disgust.

"What?" I asked, trying not to giggle.

"Olives." He faked-gagged and I burst out laughing.

"Really? You hate olives?" I raised my brow at him.

"Are you telling me you like them?"

"Actually, I adore them."

Liam picked up his fork and took one off, dumping it on the side of my plate. "Then here, they are all yours."

I watched as Liam peeled every single olive off his pizza and put them on my plate. I couldn't help but laugh as I watched his twisted face every time he flicked one off his fork.

"Is something funny to you?"

"Well, I've never seen a grown man pretty much cry over a few olives."

"Vile, nasty buggers, like a mouldy grape."

To wind him up further, I grabbed my fork, stabbed one and popped it into my mouth, moaning. Liam blinked at me.

It was then I realised that I had literally just moaned at my best friend's ex, even though I intended for it to be completely innocent. What in hell was I doing? I cleared my throat and looked away, taking a swig full of wine.

I tried to avoid eye contact for the rest of dinner, not that it worked too well. Before long, Liam and I had settled back into our unusual friendship, getting to know each other.

After we'd scoffed our faces with pizza and drank another two glasses of wine, our waiter brought over the cheque and Liam snatched it up before I could even get a glance of it.

"I'll get it to say sorry about Laura and, well, you deserve a treat after what Rob has done." He waved over the waiter again to pay as I rolled my eyes.

"Fine but, after this, we're going for drinks and the first round is on me."

"Deal."

...

We were sitting at a table for two by the door, underneath a pink neon sign that spelt 'Bra's'. Above us, hanging from the ceiling, were countless bras that people had left behind. It was a small bar; not many places to sit but it was popular. There were couples and groups in the small booth areas, with some people sitting at the bar, watching the workers make drinks with fresh fruit and a lot of alcohol.

I'd seen a lot of good things about Bra's Cocktail Bar online and so it had been on the top of my list for months. When I'd first found out that you could hang your bra on the ceiling, I'd told Laura about it straight away. We'd both planned to whip our bras off at the end of the night and get them hung up with everyone else's.

As soon as the peach daiquiri touched my lips, I couldn't help it when a little sigh escaped. Liam focused on me immediately and I blushed slightly.

"It's just good." I shrugged and looked anywhere but at Liam, who had a little smile on his face.

However, we soon realised that a problem was that the cocktails were so easy to drink that we were ordering them quicker than the barman could keep up with us. The effects of the alcohol were soon hitting me and, when I heard the opening sound of 'Into You' by Ariana Grande, I stood with a grin on my face.

"I love this song," I squealed and headed towards the dance floor. The cocktails had finally hit my brain and my newfound confidence came out in buckets. I grabbed Liam's hand on the way, not something I would have even considered if I was sober. He was warm; probably from the amount of alcohol coursing through his body.

"Esme, I don't dance," he called from behind me but I didn't care; I dragged him onto the dance floor.

"Come on; live a little, isn't that what this trip is meant to be all about?" I dropped his hand and spun on my heels, starting to sway to the music as Liam just stood there. "At least try. For *me*. Please. I thought we were friends."

"Oh, don't use that against me," he whined.

"Come on, just move your hips like this." I reached out and pulled his hips closer, forcing him to sway to the beat of the song. He tried and I gave him credit for that but he was still awful. "Okay, try this." I turned around and reached behind to grab his hands, placing them on my hips. "Move with me," I told him, tipping my head back. Liam's pupils were blown from the amount of the alcohol and sugar contents... or from how our bodies were touching in that moment. We'd spent the night with a pillow between us yet, now, we were almost pressed against each other, dancing.

Liam began to move to the music, his fingers lightly grasping my waist as I took away my hands that had been keeping them there. I moved to the rhythm of the song, singing to myself.

I couldn't remember the last time I had done this.

Rob had been bad for me; he never let me get up and dance after drinking because it was 'embarrassing' for him. With him gone, I could dance anytime I wanted to.

I was free to be myself.

And I liked that a lot.

chapter nine

Liam twirled me in his arms and I giggled. My hands landed on his chest and I looked up at him as the music thudded in our ears. There was no pillow between us now, nothing stopping our brains from crossing that final line. It was there right in front of me: a moment that could spin my entire life into a new whirlwind, a new chapter.

But it couldn't be with my best friend's ex. It was written in the stone of girl code that I was already pushing.

I pulled away and looked around for a distraction. The first thing that my drunken state thought of was to take off my favourite strapless bra and hand it to the bartender. There were cheers behind me and I laughed. Luckily, my boobs had never been an issue when it came to holding themselves up but that's because they were on the smaller side.

I turned around and Liam was standing in the middle of the dance floor like a deer caught in headlights. My little distraction had clearly given the opposite effect. I cleared my throat and readjusted my dress, before returning to the table to grab my bag. I swiped it off and rushed outside to take a breath of fresh air. Only, that didn't help clear my head as the cocktails just hit harder.

Liam wasn't far behind me. He came out the door the second my back hit the wall beside the bar.

"You feel sick?" Liam asked as if nothing had happened, as if we hadn't been about to kiss.

"A little," I lied.

"You must have been feeling hot in there? To just take off your bra?" He smirked and leaned against the wall beside me before deciding to attempt to stand alone.

I knew from that moment that he wasn't just checking on me. He felt what was going on there, what had almost happened.

"Hey, it's just what you do in there, isn't it?"

"Esme, don't beat yourself up. We're both single." Then, he began to stumble over nothing, fumbling with the wall to hold himself. He was clearly feeling as drunk as I was.

"Laura is my best friend," I told him firmly.

"She cheated on me." The audibility was barely existent.

"What?" I stood, shaking on my heels slightly. My blood ran cold. My best friend who had looked after me when *Rob* had cheated on *me*.

"I didn't tell you, thought you wouldn't believe me; she's your best friend. It's an asshole move for me to tell you now, though, so, if you want to slap me and lock me out of the hotel room, feel free. But drunk words are... are... are sober thoughts." He clicked his fingers, finally finding his words. "I know how bad you've felt about Rob and I've been feeling the same way."

It made sense why Laura hadn't told me now. In fact, she had dipped that day so quickly.

"Fuck," I whispered, brushing my hand through my hair. "I'm sorry." My eyes watered and all the feelings that I had buried during my week mopping came rushing back as I realised that Liam had been in the exact same situation. He'd spent that whole week checking in on me and sending me stupid memes and videos to try and make me smile, all while struggling himself.

"It's not your fault and I didn't tell you because… fuck, I don't know why I even told you. It was a dick move. She's your friend."

"Do you know who it was?" I pried.

"It was an old school friend. No one significant." He shrugged and looked at the floor, kicking dirt away.

"Look, I love Laura; we've been friends since we were kids. But, if she's in the wrong, then she's in the wrong." I couldn't quite believe the words coming out of my mouth but it was right. After knowing the pain of being cheated on, if she had really done it, then I couldn't stand beside her. I didn't understand how she could have done something like that when we'd bash men constantly for doing that exact thing.

I stepped forward, closing the gap between us like on the dance floor, and pressed my lips against Liam's for a single second, enough to feel the warmth and taste the peaches from the daiquiris. I pulled away, staring into his eyes; we'd swapped places and now I was the deer caught in headlights.

I saw it; I'd been blind to it. Liam was hurting, hurting as much as I was. We were feeling the same pain, the gut wrenching pain that only someone you loved could cause. I'd watched him treat my best friend like a queen and he was standing in front of me broken.

I should have seen it earlier that day when we'd made our promise. I'd also promised him that he could talk to me, tell me when he was ready. Clearly, the alcohol was helping that along.

Liam leaned forward and pressed his lips against mine again. This time, I allowed myself to feel it... with the way his stubble scratched my skin, my chest fluttered and the sound of my heartbeat thumped lightly in my ears. Our lips moved together in sync, like we were on the same page.

When Liam pulled away, I stumbled on my feet, his hands instantly attaching themselves to my waist to steady me. I reached my arms out and rested them on his shoulders. There was another moment of staring.

"What happens in Venice…" I whispered.

"Stays in Venice," he replied.

I lifted myself up and kissed him again, sweet and chaste, the alcohol completely running my brain and body.

"What's going through my head right now is no pillow wall tonight?"

And then Liam blushed. It was probably one of the sweetest things I had ever seen; a giggle escaped from my lips. "I wouldn't say no but, like, it's down to you; you're in control. You can just tell me to fuck off." Liam choked on his words.

"I'll take that into consideration. Now, take me back to the hotel before I chicken out of what stays in Venice." I smiled.

There was touching (and a lot of it) as we stumbled our way back to the hotel. We were only one alleyway away before Liam couldn't take it anymore. I was pressed against the wall, his hands sliding down, up my waist and towards the thin fabric covering my chest as his lips attached to mine and the alcohol running my adrenaline. Liam's thumb brushed my nipple and I whimpered against his lips.

"We're literally seconds away from our room."

"I don't think you understand how much I want you; is it insane of me?" he replied.

"A little." I wrapped my arms around his neck and trailed sweet kisses across his stubbled jawline. "Room. Before we sober up and come to our senses." I pushed Liam away and grabbed his hand.

I laughed, carefree and alive for the first time in months, as I pulled Liam out from the alleyway onto the Grand Canal with the Rialto bridge. It took only seconds to reach the front door of our hotel and we raced past the reception desk.

The universe gave us a sign as the lift opened: a couple stepped out and left us to get in with no time wasted. As soon as the doors shut, Liam pushed me up against the wall of the rickety lift. He grabbed one of my legs and I wrapped it around him as my dress raised to reveal my thigh. His hands gripped me there, using his thumb to make circles on my skin as I reached over and pressed the third floor button.

The lift started to move and I cupped Liam's face, pulling his lips back to mine. The desperation was higher than the amount of alcohol that was pulsing through my body. Our kisses were no longer sweet and shy; they were heated and fast. Liam's hand moved up the back of my thigh, touching the bottom of my ass. Then, the lift came to a sharp stop, jolting us and the doors open.

Liam dropped my leg, pulling me from the waist into the hallway. He took a second to look left and right, glancing to see if it was clear, before he picked me up again. Our bodies were pressed together tightly. He walked us towards our room, balancing me between the wall and his body as he reached into his pocket for the hotel keycard, all without removing his lips from mine.

As he swiped it, the door next to us opened and an elderly couple walked out. They took one look at the position we were in and rolled their eyes, muttering under their breath as they walked towards the lift. But Liam pushed open our door and carried me inside, putting me down on the bed playfully.

"I can't believe that just happened," I said, laughing in between my words and sitting up.

"Oh, we're going to be the talk of their evening." Liam smirked, dropping to his knees and starting to take off my shoes.

I blushed because, despite the fact I could now see the struggle in his jeans, Liam was still taking uttermost care with the way he was undressing me.

"At least they aren't going to see the main show."

chapter ten

"Is this main show going to start anytime soon?" I teased.

Liam threw my shoes to the side and stood, pulling off his shirt. "Once all these annoying clothes are gone."

"Okay, turn around," I told him, grasping the side zip of my dress. Liam furrowed his brows. "Look, the bra was sexy, the underwear not so much," I admitted as I dragged down the zip, holding my dress up at the front with the other hand.

"I don't care what you're wearing, Esme." He unzipped his jeans, showing off the waistband of his boxers and the straining fabric. "I just want you."

I stood and dropped my dress, my chest bare to him. My nipples were hardened from the cool air and lack of a bra or maybe from the way Liam touched me. I pushed my dress off my hips, revealing the nude colour shapewear underwear. I blushed, waiting for Liam to make some comment about how ugly the underwear was, like I'd heard before.

"Fuck, Esme." Liam swallowed. After taking a second to compose himself, he closed that small space between us and pushed me down onto the bed. I squealed as he spread my thighs with one of his knees. He didn't kiss me as I expected; instead, his lips caressed the soft tissue of my boobs. He inched closer and closer towards my nipple, then placed his soft lips around it. Liam sucked gently and there was no stopping me from tipping my head backwards and a moan escaping my lips.

My hand reached for a handful of curly hair to keep him there. While Liam lightly bit down onto my nipple, one of his hands reached down to feel the dampness on my underwear. He slipped his finger beneath the fabric and down my slit, before pushing one finger against my clit. He began rubbing slow circles that had me whimpering.

"Liam," I whined. "*Please*." My voice was cracking. What Liam was doing wasn't enough for me and I wanted more; all I could think about was how badly I needed Liam inside of me.

He hooked my underwear and pulled it down, moving just enough to be able to take it off me and throw it onto the floor.

I sat up, breathless, and leaned forwards to pull down Liam's jeans and boxers because if I was going to be naked, then so was he. I was taken back by how big he was and his dick had a slight curve that gave me the feeling it would hit all of the right places.

There was a moment where we stared at one another, admiring, before Liam reached out, cupping my cheek and brushing my hair away from my face.

"You are so beautiful." He smiled.

My cheeks flushed red and I pulled his hand away, stepping onto my tiptoes to kiss him, Liam holding my naked waist as our lips moved with more courage than there had been before.

He pushed me down onto the bed without separating us. Liam's hands moved, one to balance himself and the other slowly finding its way to where he had been. Only, this time, he pushed two fingers inside me with no trouble, my body open to him wholly. I couldn't remember the last time foreplay had been a thing when I had sex; I'd forgotten that it existed. It almost made me feel uncomfortable.

But I whimpered as Liam curled his fingers inside of me, bringing me back to the moment. He pulled away from my lips with a smirk dressing his face. Before I could even comment, he coiled his fingers again in the exact place that'd had my head rolling back into the sheets.

"Fuck," I whispered.

Liam moved position, sitting back on his knees so that his hand could press onto my lower pelvis. I gasped at the new sensation; it was beyond anything I had ever felt before. My pussy was pulsing and clenching around his fingers and that smirk was still plastered on his face as he thrusted his fingers inside of me. It didn't take long for my entire body to react, shaking, as Liam almost brought me to the edge.

Then I felt him remove his fingers and put them to his lips, sucking them to the knuckle.

"Are you sure you want to do this?" he asked me, our eyes locked.

I nodded. "Yes, yes, I want to, now. Please fuck me," I begged.

Liam leaned back, taking hold of my legs, spreading my thighs and bending my knees. I was open wide for him.

For the next few seconds, it was like everything was moving in slow motion, as the anticipation fuelled my entire body. The moment Liam slipped inside of me was euphoric. He was thicker than he looked or maybe I'd been used to something so small. He was enough to stretch me, mold my body to his. I was utterly lost in him.

Liam gripped my thighs, pulling me closer to him and deeper onto his cock. His own eyes were lit up like it was Christmas and I watched as they rolled back, his breathing only becoming more and more unsteady.

Slowly, gently, he pulled out and sharply thrusted back in. I gasped, reaching out for the bed sheets to steady myself.

"More," I mumbled, my head already spinning.

Liam found a pace, one that had us both trapped in the moment where there was just the two of us, like that was all that mattered. Each thrust sent a sharp spark of pleasure into my core.

Only moments passed until Liam leant down and pressed a domineering kiss to my lips, leaving me melting into our bed. His hands were now placed on the mattress, holding him up.

I removed my fingers from the sheets as Liam's thrusts became slow and deep, wrapping my hands around his biceps. My nails dug into his skin as the pressure in my stomach curled. Liam hissed, moaned almost, and I grinned against his lips.

I moved my hands towards his back, creating red scratches down his skin.

"Fuck, Esme. Holy shit," he groaned, pulling away. "That feels so good."

I dug them further into his back. I was surprised that sweet chef Liam had a pain kink.

It was like unleashing an animal. Liam pulled out and, within seconds, he had me flipped over, forcing me onto all fours. He grabbed my waist and I was impaled on him once more. The new angle allowed for a whole new sense of pleasure.

"I like a little pain with my pleasure, gorgeous, but do you?" Although he couldn't see me, I knew that Liam could feel my body tense. He reached out for my hair, wrapping it around his fist and pulling it back without losing his rhythm. I moaned with the flicker of pain on my scalp and the ecstasy pulsing through my entire body.

Despite being in a relationship only a couple of weeks ago, I hadn't felt this type of desire in months and I was basking in it.

"Please, Liam. I'm so close. God, I need this. Please, please, please."

His fist pulled tighter and the only sounds that filled the room were skin on skin and our uneven breaths. The four walls reeked of sex; they were painted in it.

"Come on, gorgeous, come for me. I bet you feel so good tightening around my cock."

In the need to please, the ache in my stomach released. I could feel myself around him, every ridge and vein, the swelling head deep inside of me. My moaning rattled off the walls in our room; the only thing holding me up was Liam gripping a fist full of hair.

"That's my girl; there you go, gorgeous," he praised me and a dark blush swept over my flushed skin.

I whimpered as Liam replaced his fast pace with slow and deep thrusts that sent shivers down my spine. With one final push inside of me, I could feel the muscles in his legs tighten as they were pressed almost against me. He came inside of me, filling me and groaning, enjoying the feeling.

Then Liam quickly pulled out.

"Shit, I am so sorry. Are you even on anything? Oh I'm such a twat."

I rolled over, clenching my pussy to stop it covering our sheets.

"Hey, you're good," I spoke, dazed. "I'm on the injection. Don't worry. And well... guess I know where you've been and all that." I looked away from him. "I'm going to clean up." I quickly shuffled off the bed and ran to the toilet. My head was woozy from the orgasm and the cocktails.

I cleaned up and, when I entered the room again, Liam was already laying in bed. Without a second thought, I climbed in beside him, no pillow wall, and his arm draped over me.

The exhaustion and alcohol sent me into a deep sleep.

chapter eleven

I don't know what hit me worse, the headache or the guilt, when I opened my eyes to the sun shining through the window. I was facing the naked body of Liam beside me, with no pillow wall in sight. I felt sick to my stomach and I couldn't put my finger on why that was either.

Without trying to make a sound, I slowly moved out of bed. Luckily, a pair of leggings and my hoodie were dumped at the side of the bed: my getaway outfit waiting for me. Quickly and quietly, I put on my clothes and grabbed my bag from last night, then my trainers.

I made my escape from the room and, once I was in the clear by the lift, I was able to finally breathe. The memories of last night were running through my head. Liam had called me gorgeous and hadn't ridiculed me for my shapewear. Then, on the other hand, I had to remember that he was my best friend's ex.

Keeping my head down, I stepped out of the lift and turned left towards the hotel restaurant. The place was packed with people taking advantage of the free breakfast but I managed to find myself a small table in the corner with a little window, where I could see the Rialto bridge. I placed my phone on the table to note that someone was there and quickly grabbed myself a glass of orange juice and a croissant, sitting back down a moment later, only to pick at the flakes of pastry.

I'd fucked up.

Really fucked up.

I needed to get the next flight home; what else could I do? So, I picked up my phone, searching for the cheapest last-minute flights; I didn't care if I had to spend the day in the airport. I just *had* to go home.

Before I could check the fourth search result on my phone, it rang.

Laura's name was lighting up the screen.

I couldn't avoid her much longer either so I tucked my messy hair behind my ears, as if she could see me, and answered her call.

"Hey."

"There you are. I was trying to get hold of you."

"Sorry. I was sightseeing all day then I crashed in my hotel." Then fucked your ex boyfriend, that you hadn't even told me is your ex. That you had also cheated on while bashing mine for doing the exact same.

"I wanted to check in;, your mom said you booked a last minute trip to Venice. And I was like, that's weird, considering everything."

"Yeah, I decided that I shouldn't let the single life stop me from living my *actual* life. But I'm feeling home sick so I'll probably be back tomorrow."

"So, have you heard from Rob?" she asked.

"He's tried calling but I don't want to talk to him. Hey, do you think you can go get my things from his house? I just can't."

"Yeah, of course. You know I'd do anything for you."

I caught a glimpse of Liam heading towards me on the other side of the room. Entering panic mode, I stumbled on my words.

"So, I'm gonna... I need to finish eating and then think about what I'm gonna do. So, catch you later?"

"Yeah, text me. Love you."

"Love you too." I ended the call the moment that Liam stood in front of my table, before sitting down opposite me.

"Esme..."

"Don't. We were drunk. It was a mistake. It's over and I'm going to head home."

"You don't have to do that." He shook his head but I couldn't tell if it was sadness or pity in his eyes. Either way, I couldn't let it influence my decision, not after how long it took me to make it.

"I do. I broke the biggest girl code rule and I can't forgive myself for that."

"Look, you don't have to go. We can still enjoy the trip. We agreed that what happened in Venice would stay in Venice so why can't we just stay in our bubble? This was meant to be our break from all the shit back home. And, if I'm honest, I prefer being around you more than anyone at home." Liam held up his hands innocently; he wasn't going to change his mind about this. "I'm not going to make any moves, not unless you want me to and it's clear that you don't. So, we're just friends."

"Okay and maybe we should try and see if they'll give us that spare room again. Then there can be no more accidents."

"I'll go ask while you shower. I thought we could check out Murano?"

"Yeah, sure."

...

The guilt didn't wash away when I stepped under the hot steaming water. I was stained in it. I also knew I wasn't ready to face whatever was waiting for me back home. Rinsing the cocktails out of my hair made me feel slightly better and, when I stepped out,

I promised myself that I would at least try to enjoy the rest of my holiday.

I wiped away the condensation on the bathroom mirror, catching a glimpse of my wet hair, when my phone rang. Rob's name flashed across the cracked screen and, this time, I answered it.

"What?" I snapped.

"I've been trying to call you for days."

"Then why can't you get the picture that we have nothing to talk about?"

"Where are you? Laura said you left town for a few days."

"Is that all you have to say? Tell me Rob, who was she? Or can you not even admit that?"

"It was... it was someone from work," he stumbled out.

"Then why don't you go bother her?" I snapped.

"Go on, your turn. Who are you on holiday with? I know you, you wouldn't go alone."

"It's none of your business anymore. You have no right. Go and fuck the brunette that I found in your bed, Rob, and leave me alone," I shouted and hung up, sliding my phone across the counter so hard that it bounced off the wall, then into the sink.

I needed to get out of the hotel and get myself a glass of wine soon as possible.

After drying myself off, I put on a pair of jeans and a white button up shirt, then wrapped my hair into a towel.

Stepping into the room, I saw Liam packing his clothes into his bag. He looked up when he heard me.

"Hey, so there's a room just three doors down that they've moved me into. Free of charge because the booking got messed up. Looks like we caught the manager this time."

"That's great." I mustered a smile.

"I'll go dump this and then get dressed. The boats run every half an hour over to Murano."

"Perfect, I'll meet you outside the hotel? I think I'm going to go grab some gelato." I picked up my brush and pulled the towel off my head, starting to untangle the mess of blonde knots.

"Are you okay? I heard you shouting."

Swallowing, I pushed my hair back from my face and looked at Liam. Nice, kind Liam, from the moment I met him. Maybe in another life I would have gotten *his* number on that night out, instead of Rob's, and I wouldn't have been in the mess that I was.

"I was sick of him trying to call me. I answered and he acted like nothing had happened. I don't have time to listen. After all, we're meant to be getting away from it all, right?"

"Exactly." Liam saw right through my fakery because his smile had pity written all over it. "I'll see you soon, yeah? I'm just three doors down if you need anything."

"Thank you."

Liam bowed his head and left the room.

His half was bare, even more so with the lack of pillow barrier in the middle of the bed. I couldn't help but stare at the mess of sheets as I brushed through the rest of my hair, sweeping it back into a low bun at the base of my neck.

Soon after, I grabbed my bag off the desk, along with my keycard. Taking myself down into the lobby and outside of the hotel, I was glad to breathe the fresh scent of bakeries and salt water. No one was wrong when they said Venice smelled awful but that was in the back streets, not the bustling grand canal where the Rialto bridge was already getting its first rounds of photos for the day.

There was a small gelato place a couple of buildings down, with a hole in the wall pizza place. After picking one scoop of orange and another of lemon gelato, I sat down on the steps leading into the canal by Rialto bridge and began spooning the ice-cream into my mouth.

Sugar made everything better.

Though, something told me it wasn't the only thing that would.

"Enjoying the view?"

I jumped and looked over my shoulder to see Liam, who had got dressed up in a pair of white linen trousers and blue button up. His hair was messily tucked behind his ears and his casual look didn't help me feel 'casual' in the slightest.

"If I could stay here forever, I would."

Liam held out his hand; I went to take it then pulled back.

"Esme, come on, I'm not going to bite."

"Yeah, of course. Sorry." Flashes of the night before came to mind when our palms touched. Liam wasn't going to hurt me but I wasn't so sure that I wouldn't hurt *him*, while throwing myself further into the pits of guilt.

chapter twelve

There was an awkward silence as we walked the fifteen minutes to vaporetto stop that would take us to Murano. Even though we weren't talking, our hands were almost touching. I tried to distract myself with the shops that we passed by, the refreshing breeze brushing through my hair and the vibrant colours of glass ornaments in the windows.

"You okay?" Liam nudged me.

"Yeah, of course. Just taking in the views. There's so much for such a small island."

Liam's eyes were glimmering like he had just walked out of a romance movie. It was like seeing him in a whole new light, one that I never considered he could be under.

"Anything you want to see on Murano?" he asked as we came to the stop. There was a small crowd of people ready to cram themselves onto the waterbus, the same as us.

"Maybe we can catch a glass demo somewhere too? It is the glass island, after all."

"I was thinking the same thing. We should have booked one of those workshops."

"Oh my god, no. I can see it now: just this deformed blob of glass that was meant to look like a cat or something," I told him, laughing.

"It could be an abstract piece. Those are the art pieces that sell the most, right?" Liam smirked as we walked up to the ticket machine.

I watched as he selected two day tickets, almost opening my mouth to stop him and tell him I would buy my own, then reconsidering when I imagined the very public and awkward conversation it could end in. Liam tapped his phone on the machine and the tickets printed out.

When he handed over mine, our fingers touched a little and my cheeks burned red. I refused to make eye contact as I thanked him and turned towards the crowd. I was thankful as the vaporetto turned up and there was no time to say anything else as everyone began to move.

As we stepped onto the floating platform with everyone else, I scanned my ticket to validate it. Liam was right behind me as we shuffled along with the crowd.

On the boat, I made the way down to the end where there was a small section of seats. There were a few free, most people hiding from the wind inside. I sat down and turned to rest my arm on the railing, getting a better view. Liam sat next to me, slouching down and looking around.

I watched the water flurry around the boat as it moved away from the stop. The further we went from the main island, the brighter the blue of the water became. I reached for my phone in my bag, wanting to take a snapshot of the view, only it wasn't there.

I'd left it in the bathroom.

"Oh, for fuck's sake," I groaned.

"What's up?"

"I left my phone back at the hotel after my argument with Rob." I leaned my head on my hand, trying to think how I'd even managed that.

"You can use mine for photos if you want to take any."

"I don't have my bank card either. I was going to use my Apple Pay." I looked over at Venice which seemed to be floating further and further away; there was no way of getting back to the hotel.

"Esme, you're fine. I have mine and we can just sort it out later, don't worry." Liam laughed at my panic. "Part of me wishes I'd forgotten mine too. Maybe you'll enjoy the peace and quiet."

"Hmmm, guess you're right. A day without having to reject Rob's calls would be therapeutic."

"Which is what this trip is all about."

I held out my hand. "Phone? I'll get some pictures of Venice from here."

Liam pulled it out of his pocket and placed it in my hand. His screen lit up and I noticed that the anniversary picture of him and Laura was gone. Even after what we had done together, the thought of Liam and Laura no longer being a couple was a strange feeling, especially after almost three years of my friend non-stop yapping about him. I wanted to ask what had happened. Ask either of them. I knew it was down to Laura cheating, my best friend wasn't close to any kind of perfection, but I just had this gut feeling that something was missing. That there was something else that Liam hadn't told me yet.

I took some pictures of the boat leaving Venice behind, trying not to think about what Laura had done, then handed Liam back his phone. As we were only going to Murano, the trip was just fifteen minutes. We passed them in mostly silence and with a few odd comments here and there about the views we were seeing as we crossed the crystal blue sea.

Nothing could compare to the beauty that Venice and Murano's buildings held; the artistic infrastructure would forever have my heart. Tall, handcrafted homes and businesses that had been made with the passion and love that Italy was known for.

As the vaperetto pulled up to the island, we stood to get a better view. It had a similar aesthetic to Venice, with varying colours of bare brick. I suspected some of the vibrant rainbow buildings I had read about were further inland.

I followed Liam off the boat and we stepped aside from the crowd of tourists that exited with us. Liam pulled out his phone, tapping away at his keyboard for a moment, then he looked up and glanced around, his pretty hair swishing with him.

"So, I think we need to go this way?" He pointed without even looking up from his map. "That's where all the colourful buildings are on the canal."

Once we began to walk further into Murano, I began to recognise the things I'd seen online, the hues of reds, blues and yellows scattered across the architecture, making me think I was in an Italian adaptation of *Balamory*.

One thing I noticed straight away was that there were more locals on the island than in Venice, giving it a calming tone of Italian that echoed the streets as we walked around.

We were almost touching again as we strolled side by side, except I stopped when I spotted a glass store that had their workshop in view from the main window.

"Wait," I called, reaching out for his arm. "Look." I cleared my throat, dropping my hand as Liam turned and watched the glass maker as he used his tools to mold the molten glass into a vase. We watched intently as the various colours merged with one another, creating a beautiful glass vase, an array of red, blue and yellow, just like the buildings.

"Looks like it's a shop too," Liam spoke, looking towards the door, where you could see a sneak peak of the glass collection.

"Come on, let's go inside." Instinctively, I took his hand like an excited child, not even taking a moment to think what I was doing as I pulled us into the store. It was huge and must have crossed onto the other side of the alley as well.

Shelving covered all of the walls, even across the windows that managed to catch the lights in just the way for the colours to bounce off the white walls. Desperate to see more, I let go of Liam's hand as I wandered down the aisle, admiring all of the pieces of glass art. Vases, decorations, plates and cups: everything you could possibly make.

I caught eyes with the cashier, a middle-aged woman, with greying hair at the roots. She smiled at me and I awkwardly returned one as I stopped in front of a stained glass window that was hanging from the ceiling. A small but peaceful sigh escaped my lips as I heard a camera shutter.

Whipping my hair, I looked to the side where Liam stood with his phone out.

It was pointed directly at me.

"The rule was no pictures." I crossed my arms.

"The rule was no pictures *together* and you don't have your phone. So, I took one for you. I'll send it to you right now and delete it."

"Let me see," I said, stepping towards him, tucking into his side.

Liam pulled up his gallery and clicked on the photo of me. I looked happy, peaceful, the colours bouncing off my skin and clothes while I admired the stained glass.

"Hmm."

"You like it." He smirked. "See, no rules broken."

"No *more* rules broken, more like," I mumbled.

"Stop beating yourself up, please," he whispered.

Looking up at him, I saw the sad look in his eye. I'd been non-stop talking negatively about what we had done, not even considering that his feelings were bruised.

I cleared my throat.

"You were good. I enjoyed it, you know?" My cheeks burned red as I admitted to him how good he had made me feel. There was no denying it. I was just awful with how to say it. And I probably shouldn't have come out with it in public.

"I enjoyed it too."

Silent seconds passed by. And, in those seconds, our faces drifted closer together until he was almost in reach. My heart was beating faster at the thought of being able to taste his morning coffee on his lips and the urge to indulge myself in him was stronger than before

I forced my eyes shut and stepped away, turning towards a shelf of trinkets. A little red glass gondola sat there amongst the other ornaments. Picking it up, I held it to the light.

"This is cute. I'm going to grab this for my mom." I didn't give him a chance to speak as I walked towards the woman at the till. "Just this, please."

She pulled out a piece of bubble wrap to roll it up and then placed it into a paper bag, the little gift ones without handles.

"That will be eighteen euros," she spoke, with a thick Italian accent.

"Card, please." Liam stepped behind me.

I stupidly forgot that he was also the only one with money and I hadn't escaped as the smell of his aftershave filled my nostrils again.

"You two make a lovely couple."

"Oh, we're not..."

Liam cut me off. "Grazie." He smiled at her, as I picked up my gift and slipped it into my bag.

I stepped around Liam and walked towards the closest door that led us to the alley over from where we were. Taking deep breaths once the fresh air hit, I tried to calm myself down. I heard the bell from the door opening and knew Liam had joined me.

"It's almost lunch," he spoke simply.

"Yeah. Sounds good." I edged away, leaving a gap between us, the way that it should be.

We wandered some more, taking ourselves onto the main canal, where a few of the restaurants were beginning to open for the lunch rush. I noticed a particular one with an outside area that went onto the water, with fencing around it and a frame where beautiful handcrafted baubles hung from it in various colours and sizes.

"How about here?" I asked.

"Yeah, it looks good."

The host waiting outside for passers by had already heard us and approached to seat us.

"Beautiful day to sit outside for a beautiful couple," he said.

I went to open my mouth and correct him but decided to keep it shut instead. Seemed like everyone thought we were together.

He reached out his arm and pointed towards the seats; they were in the corner, where we would be the closest to the water.

He placed menus on the table and we sat down. I shuffled my seat closer to the table and picked up a menu, taking a quick flick through.

"Do you know what you would like to drink?" he asked, pulling a pad and pen from his pocket.

"Your house white wine and I'll have an Italian beer, please," Liam answered.

The host bowed slightly and turned away to head inside.

"How did you know I wanted wine?" I raised my brow.

"Because you love wine and I didn't think you'd want to touch a cocktail after how many we had last night because I sure don't."

I should have been annoyed that Liam had ordered for me but I wasn't.

Why wasn't I?

Even Rob had always let me order my own but Liam just clearly knew me. Already. It was a refreshing change, I think. I liked it. Liam was the kind of person that I needed in my life, someone that just understood me and wanted to learn more about me, put the effort in like I did for him.

"Thank you." I meant it. I really did.

"I got you, Es." He picked up his menu.

'Es.'

It sounded nice coming from his lips. It was hard not to hang onto everything that made my heart flutter. Things were starting to change between us. How could they not? But I couldn't let them. No matter what Laura had done, I couldn't fall in love with her ex.

"What are you thinking about what to eat? They have some classic pasta dishes on here. Ugh, lasagne. Hate the stuff." He faked gagging playfully, just like he had with the olives, and I couldn't help but laugh at his silly face.

"Yeah, me too."

Fucking lasagne.

chapter thirteen

I thought I was going to feel more relaxed with having the hotel room to myself. Instead, I was rattling. I'd cleaned everything, taken a shower and then decided to have a bath too.

Afterwards, I lay on the bed, spreading out my limbs like a starfish and letting out a huge sigh. Only, the silence was deafening and the room was too empty.

Trying to ignore my stupid feelings, I curled up under the sheets and scrolled TikTok on my battered and smashed phone. Even with the entire bed to myself, I stayed on my half of the mattress. The side that Liam had slept in was untouched after the maid had changed the sheets.

I reached out to trace my fingers over the cold sheets.

"I'm going to hell," I whispered to myself, then threw off the bed sheets. Taking my hoodie from my case, I pulled it over my head as I walked towards the door, snatching the keycard from the desk.

The hallway was a ghost town and I was grateful because my hoodie basically made me look naked on my bottom half. I wrapped my arms around myself, walking three down doors down to where Liam's new room was.

Chewing on my lip, I knocked at the door and waited.

Liam was taken back to see me standing there. I was taken back to see him dressed in just a pair of shorts, the faint line of his abs on show, along with the v line that disappeared underneath. I cleared my throat.

"So, it turns out it's kinda boring in the room without someone else there. Without *you* there," I fumbled.

"I was going to try and find something to watch but it's all Italian. However, I do have a large amount of chocolate that I should share with someone." Liam stepped aside to let me in and I took him up on the offer.

His new room was similar to the other one, except it was slightly smaller with a double bed, rather than king size. The TV was switched onto the news and I couldn't understand a word of it.

On the bed, there were various editions of Kinder chocolate, along with a few wrappers. I sat on the edge as Liam threw himself down, making me bounce a little on the mattress.

"It's boiling in here," he spoke. "I'm assuming you have something on underneath your hoodie, so you don't have to just sit there in it."

I swallowed.

"What if... What if I didn't?" I asked. Liam's eyes went wide. "Sorry, I shouldn't have said it like that." I shook my head and went to stand up but he reached out and grabbed my wrist.

"If you didn't, I'd devour you, Es. I don't think I'd ever be able to stop."

"That's all I can think about. Which is wrong of me because of Laura."

"You need to stop feeling guilty because I guarantee she doesn't feel guilty about what she did while we were *in* a relationship."

"Do you promise this isn't you trying to get one over on her?" I sat back down, willing to at least hear him out.

"I want you for no other reason than I want you, Esme. Just you. Which is mind boggling because I've never seen you that way until now."

I pulled my hoodie over my head, my vest and shorts didn't leave a lot to the imagination. Dropping it on the floor, Liam swiped his sweet treats off the bed.

"Come here," he ordered, laying on his back.

I slowly crawled across the bed. When I was close enough, Liam pulled me to straddle his waist. I looked down at him, my hair falling around my face.

"While we're here, it's just us."

"*Just us*. We can be whatever we want," I whispered. "And I think I want it to be us."

"I want that too. What happens in Venice…"

"…Stays in Venice."

I leaned down and pressed our lips together. I'd missed the taste of him. Denying him in Murano, taking myself away from the temptation, had been difficult, especially because I wanted him so much. I'd never thought about him this way either, not until this trip, and I didn't want to stop. And I didn't have to in our bubble.

Liam's hands gripped my waist, pushing my ass down onto his hard length under his shorts. Grinding my hips, I deepened our kiss, devouring one another. He moved one hand to slip under my bottoms and grabbed my cheeks tightly. A small moan escaped my lips and I pulled away. All I could see in his eyes was hunger.

"I'm dying to taste you, Esme. Are you going to let me?"

My timid nod was all he needed to flip us over and yank my PJs from my waist and pull at the vest.

"Off."

I lifted my upper body and took it off, discarding it across the room.

My breathing was shallow as I lay naked in front of him and it wasn't the first time. However, it *was* the first time doing it while sober. I was more nervous than last night but I knew that I wanted him, even though I shouldn't.

Liam moved lower down the bed, his face directly in front of my bare pussy, then moved closer and closer, not breaking eye contact with me. He used one hand to spread me open and teased my clit.

Shivers ran down my spine as it woke up. Liam wrapped his lips around it, sucking softly. I reached out for the bed sheet either side of me, digging my fingers in the patterned fabric.

"Liam," I breathed. "Shit."

Liam brushed his tongue inside of me and I closed my eyes as every nerve in my body set on fire. He didn't answer me but, instead, pushed two fingers inside of me while eating me out. I tangled my own tighter into the sheets, whimpers turning into moans.

"Good girl. I want to hear you, gorgeous." He lifted his head to speak. But then his face disappeared again, eating me out like time was running out.

There was no way to hold back the moans that became screams as he nipped on my hard clit, hard enough to send me over the edge. I came onto his face and Liam lapped up every drip of wetness between my legs. When he came up for air, he wiped his mouth with the back of his hand, a smile dancing on his lips and his cock rock solid in his shorts.

"Why am I the only one naked?" I spoke, breathless.

"Why don't you fix it then?" Liam kneeled.

Pulling myself onto my knees, I reached for the waistband to tug down his shorts. Once his cock was freed, I could admire the pre cum that was leaking from the tip.

I darted out my tongue, tasting it. Glancing up to look him in the eye, I wrapped my lips around the head of his cock. His eyes rolled back in pleasure.

"Fuck, Esme," he groaned and I took him deeper into my mouth.

What I couldn't fit, I wrapped my hand around, sliding up and down.

Liam's hand wove into my hair, forcing my mouth down a little further, making him whimper like he had made me.

I swirled my tongue around the underside of his tip and his grip on my hair tightened as he hissed.

"That's it, gorgeous. Keep going."

I bobbed my head faster, almost gagging on the length of him. He pulled harder at my hair as the sympathy of Liam's moans echoed off the walls. His hips buckled slightly against my mouth as his hand completely dropped.

"I want to fill your pretty mouth so much but I need to fill your pussy so much more." His words were barely audible as he pulled me off his cock, using his fingers to lift my chin so I would look at him. The dazed smile only grew as he swiped his thumb over my swollen lips.

"Are you gonna just stare at me? Or are you going to fuck me like you said?" I whispered, wrapping my lips around his thumb and sucking lightly.

Liam fisted around his cock, touching himself as he watched.

"How do you want me to have you?" he asked. My lips made a popping sound as I removed them from his thumb.

"What way have you been thinking about having me?"

I didn't know what to do when he climbed off the bed and turned off the light. The TV was the only reason I could faintly see him.

"Come to the window," he spoke and I immediately got up from the bed.

Rob shouldn't have crossed my mind while being with Liam but I couldn't help but think about the lack of excitement Rob always gave me. Liam was leaving me with questions, quite literally keeping me in the dark, which only made me feel warm between my thighs.

I could barely make him out as he opened the wooden window panels, revealing the streets of Venice. Once I was close by, he also switched off the TV, leaving us in complete darkness as he grabbed me by the waist.

"I can't stop thinking about fucking you right by this window. It crossed my mind that first morning. If Venice is the only place that I can have you, then I want you to remember it every time you think about the view. How I bent you over and fucked you without a soul noticing down there." He pressed his lips against mine, tasting one another. I felt him take off his shorts completely, his hard length touching my skin.

I didn't want our kiss to end and I moaned as he pulled away. His response was to spin me around to face the glass. He placed my hands on the window sill and I heard the drag of the desk close by. Liam lifted my leg onto it, spreading me into the perfect position. All I could hear were my shallow breaths as I took in the lights of the restaurants, who were serving tourists their dinner, couples and groups taking photos on the bridge in the dark, with no idea that I was about to be fucked.

Liam had been right.

It would be all I would remember when I thought about this view. Everytime I would take in the sights, all I'd think about was the way Liam had touched me.

Gliding down the curve of my ass, his hands took in each inch.

"Look at everyone, Esme. They don't have a clue that you're going to be screaming my name." A slap landed on my ass.

I felt him move closer behind me, the tip of his cock dragging down my ass and then hovering over the opening of my pussy. I whined as he pushed slowly inside of me. his fingers digging into my skin, almost bruising me, and I didn't think I would have minded if he did.

The pace was slow, Liam's groans matching mine as I supported my body the best I could manage. He was holding back, teasing me.

People below us really had no clue what we were doing and the thought only made me wetter. With each thrust, I became louder.

"Are you steady?" he questioned.

"Yeah," I managed to breath out, creating steam on the window pane in front of me.

Liam's next thrust was harder and the angle he had put me in ensured I felt every inch of him. I released a surprised whimper as my breasts were pushed against the window sill and then he pulled out as fast he had thrusted inside of me, our bodies slapping together.

He still used one hand to balance me but the other snaked around to find my throbbing clit. The circles moved as fast as he was fucking me. There was no possible way to hold back my screams and moans as the window steamed up further.

"Liam!" I cried out.

"Do you want to come around my cock, my gorgeous girl? What do you think they would say down there if they knew you were getting fucked in the window like a slut?"

I moaned in response to his words.

"You like that too? You surprise me, Esme. You always seemed like such a sweet, innocent girl."

I shook my head, not that he could see.

"Come for me, gorgeous. I want to feel you tighten around my cock."

Between the steamed window and my vision blurring from pleasure, I could only see lights spotted on the other side of the glass. I whimpered his name as I pushed back against him, begging for more with my body because I could barely make out his name.

The pressure burst inside of me and I tightened around his hard cock as I came, a soft whine escaping from my lips. Liam didn't stop there. He continued thrusting inside of me and removed his hand from my clit.

"Fucking hell, Esme. Shit." He growled as he buried himself deep into my trembling body. Each time he was inside of me, he stayed that little bit longer, deep, until I felt the rush of hot cum fill my pussy.

I sighed in pleasure, resting my head on my arms.

Liam slowly removed himself from me, hissing from the sensitivity. He helped me lower my shaking legs as his cum ran down them. He then shut the window panes as I made a dash for the bathroom in the dark, closing the door slightly and flicking the light on.

Sitting down on the toilet, I cleaned myself up with tissue.

"You okay?" he called in.

"Yeah," I chuckled. "Is it okay if I take a shower?"

"Yeah, of course. Just let me know if you need anything."

I got into the shower, then started to wash myself down. Turning around to grab the body wash was the moment I realised that Liam's was the only one available. I popped open the cap and inhaled the musky scent, sighing to myself.

I was more screwed than the night before.

Because now I was starting to like Liam more than I thought I ever could.

Now, he looked like someone I could love.

And someone I really shouldn't.

chapter fourteen

When I woke up, the guilt was still there but less strong. I still thought that I was an awful person, even with the smile on my face as I woke up in Liam's arms. Our bare skin was pressed together, slightly sweaty. Noticing that his hand was firmly cupping my breast as he snored softly, I laughed lightly.

It seemed to stir him. Liam groaned and rolled over in the bed, allowing me to turn over to admire him.

His brown curls were frizzy and voluminous on his pillows, his lips parted. I reached out and brushed some of the curls from his face and his eyes fluttered open. When he spotted it was me, a smile danced on his lips.

"Morning," he croaked.

It was different to the other mornings; there was no awkwardness polluting the air, only the soft sounds of Venice waking up and our breathing. His hand crept up my bare waist under the covers.

"Are you okay?" The real question he was asking was 'Are you going to run again?'.

"I'm okay. There's really no turning back now," I whispered, laying my head on the pillow.

"Does that mean I can kiss you?" he asked.

There was a moment of silence before I nodded. Liam's hand moved up to cup my face, pulling me closer so our lips met, despite our morning breath.

The kiss was soft, fitting for the early summer hours. There was no denying that my heart fluttered, his fingers wrapping around the back of my head and knotting into my hair. The softness soon ended and the hunger from the night before started to peek through. He pulled away.

"Mmmm, part of me wants to keep you all to myself in this room."

Our foreheads rested against each other and all I could hear was the sound of our faltering breathing.

"How about we order room service and at least spend a few hours together?"

"I've never heard a more perfect idea." He pecked my lips.

"But, for now, I think both of us need to shower, perhaps together?" My cheeks burned red.

"I hope you mean what I think you do because I could do with a little help." He smirked.

I raised my brow, reaching my hand under the covers for his hard cock and wrapping my fingers around it, lightly squeezing.

"I'm sure I can do something about that," I told him, letting go and climbing out of the bed so he could see my naked body. I smirked, making my way to the bathroom. The window caught my eye for a split second, warmth sprending between my thighs as I remembered how Liam had fucked me there the night before. I could hear light footsteps behind me as I switched on the light.

Liam stood behind me in the mirror and I smiled at him teasingly; it was short lived as he grabbed my hips and bent me forwards over the bathroom counter.

"You have a thing about bending girls over, huh?" I had to expel the thought of Laura from my mind as soon as it appeared.

"No, that just happens to be you and your peachy ass, gorgeous." A light slap landed on my cheeks, bucking me forwards. With one hand still on my hips, Liam reached open and flicked the shower on. "And you look absolutely stunning when you come, do you want to see?" Liam pressed his morning wood against me as I braced myself on the counter.

"Please." I blushed, looking at him in the mirror.

Liam knocked my legs apart so he could slip his hard cock into me. I was slightly wet but, as soon as he was deep inside of me, it was like opening flood gates. I moaned as he dragged his length out.

"Slow or fast? Pick," he groaned as he thrusted back inside me.

"Hard, fuck me hard. Girls are just as horny as you men in the morning, you know?" I spoke, teasing him.

Liam's fingers dug into my left hip as his right hand tangled in my hair, forcing me to look at myself in the mirror. I'd never seen the slutty look in my eye as I was getting fucked before and the way my lips parted.

Liam's pace increased and he hissed as he hit the right spot for us both.

"Fuck," I moaned, the pain in my scalp only adding to the pleasure in my stomach. I must have been so vain because looking at myself in the mirror was helping my orgasm find the edge to throw itself off.

For a moment, I watched Liam, his curls bouncing as he fucked me. It was all I needed to scream as the mirror started to steam up from the shower. My pussy tightened and Liam groaned, clearly holding back from filling me up. He released my hair and spun me around, lifting me onto the counter. I was pulled forwards and I balanced myself with my hands as Liam slipped between my wet thighs again.

"Now you've seen how beautiful you are, I can kiss you." His kissed me as he grinded his hips, slowly fucking me for a moment, before gathering his energy and going again.

I nipped his lip and whined at the sensitivity running through my core.

"I want to feel you fill me up." I enjoyed it far more than I wanted to admit, more than I thought I would.

Liam tucked his head against the nape of my neck as he rutted into me, losing rhythm, completely lost in fucking me as hard as he could.

Then, with one final thrust, he came inside of me, like he had done twice before. Our breathing was out of sync but our foreheads pressed together in unison as a small moan escaped my lips.

"Being with you feels better and better each time," Liam spoke as he pulled his dick from my full pussy.

"I can agree on that." But I shouldn't have.

"Think you can stand?" Liam smirked and, in return, I whacked him on the arm.

"Talk about having an ego. Yes, I can stand." I balanced myself on his shoulder and slid off the counter, the cum already starting to run down my legs. I headed for the hot shower to wash myself down.

Liam stepped in with me, reaching over for the soap as I stood under the hot water. Closing my eyes,

I sighed under the jets. I felt the washcloth on my back and shoulder, lathering my skin with the scent of him.

"Want me to wash your hair?" he asked.

I nearly melted there and then. Washing someone's hair was intimate and caring, something I didn't have done unless I was getting my roots touched up.

"I'd like that," I admitted, leaning back against him as the washcloth trailed towards my front and bubbled up my breasts.

"Here, take this and then wet your hair for me."

I took it from him, then turned around to face him, letting my head fall back under the shower to drench my hair. Liam grabbed his shampoo and squirted some into the palm of his hand, rubbing it in his hands, massaging my scalp.

"Mmm, that feels good," I spoke.

"I like that you smell like me."

"Do you have any conditioner?" I asked, glancing at him.

Liam chuckled. "I have curly hair; of course I do."

"Good because my hair gets so dry."

"Don't worry, your hair will be smooth and shiny," he told me and I smiled. "Tip your head back so we can wash this out."

Having someone take care of me was relaxing. I knew that Liam was kind; I'd always seen that. He was the total opposite of Rob, who wouldn't even care to make me a cup of tea in the morning. I'd missed out on the small and sweet things that whole time and hadn't even noticed. The pain of being cheated on hadn't gone yet but I was slowly coming to the realisation that maybe there were better people out in the world than him.

People like Liam.

People that cared.

He put a dollop of coconut conditioner in his hand, then started to run it through my mids and ends. I continued to wash my body while he did that, relaxing into his touch.

Once it was rubbed in, his hand snaked around the back of my neck and pulled me into a kiss. I wrapped my arms around his neck, washcloth still in my hand, as I enjoyed the sweet touch of his lips against mine. We pulled away at the same time, looking into one another's eyes.

"If this is only for a few more days, will you let me take you out today?" Liam asked.

I chewed my lip, taking a moment to consider, before nodding. Liam kissed me again and my knees went weak.

"Good because I want you to smile until your face aches."

"I already am and that's because of you."

chapter fifteen

I smelled like him. Even my PJ's were clinging to the fragrance of coconut and lynx.

After putting back on my clothes, I turned to look at Liam, who was leaning against the wall in nothing but a towel, his eyes trained on me. I took a moment to admire his faint abs and v line, his wet curls pushed back behind his ears.

"How do I need to dress?" The excitement was bubbling inside of me; I couldn't remember the last time I'd had a date with Rob.

"Anyway you like but I think you deserve a little romance. And I want to romance you." He smiled, taking a piece of my wet hair and twirling it around his finger, his head tilted to one side, admiring me. My cheeks turned pink and were hot to touch.

I nodded and reached for the handle. "Okay, so cute? I can do cute," I told him and opened the door to head back to my room. I walked back down the corridor and pulled my keycard from my hoodie pocket.

The emptiness still made me feel uneasy but I took my time to get ready. I dried my hair, using my straighteners to curl it, and then pulled out my light blue, floral sundress, pairing it with my strapless bra. Before putting on my makeup, I checked the weather to see how it was going to be so I didn't sweat it all off.

While I was applying my face, there was a knock on the door and I stood to open it, seeing Liam on the other side. He was wearing a white t-shirt and blue jeans and yet still looked smart. His curls were now dried into ringlets, with his sunglasses perched on his head.

He stared at me, leaning on the door frame.

"Esme, you look beautiful."

"Thank... thank you." I wasn't sure where the flood of nerves came from as he stood in front of me, looking way too hot for his own good. "So, what are we doing?"

"First, we're gonna go to that cafe next door for breakfast and the rest is a secret."

"Really, Liam?" I raised an eyebrow, grabbing my bag and remembering my phone this time. The last thing I wanted was to be left phoneless, again.

"Really." He held out his hand and it took me a moment to accept it. I couldn't remember the last time I'd held hands with someone other than Zoe or Laura.

Liam didn't let go of me as he directed us towards the lift and pressed the button; the doors opened ten seconds later and we stepped in. I caught a glimpse of us in the mirror and hated to admit that we looked good together. Though, I couldn't allow myself to think too much about us when it was only in Venice that we could be together.

The lift doors opened on the reception floor and we stepped out, hand in hand. We headed for the cafe next door which worked as a bar at night. The tables outside had been set out with little vases and flowers; they were still in the shade which made it slightly chilly but I didn't mind it because of the view we had of the canal. It would never get old.

Liam and I sat down at one of the tables and I turned to face the water.

"So, turns out this is more like lunch than breakfast," Liam spoke up, taking a glance at his watch.

"That's okay, I guess we were both tired." My cheeks burned red as I looked over at him.

Liam offered me a cocky lopsided smirk. "How are you enjoying the view today?" He leaned back in his chair and crossed his leg over.

I rolled my eyes at him. "Shut up. I can't even believe you did that." Picking up the menu, I shook my head.

Liam shrugged his shoulders, smirking. "And I'd do it again."

My cheeks bloomed brighter and I buried my head into the menu, trying to decide what to eat. There was the classic pasta and pizza but I needed a change. My heart could have leaped when I saw the British classic.

"Definitely going to have jacket potato with cheese and beans," I spoke, changing the subject from how Liam had fucked me in a window last night.

"I appreciate the simplicity. I might go for the cheese and ham toastie. I'll go in and order. Don't even attempt to try and give me cash."

"Hmm," I replied, planning to just transfer him the money later, like I had to yesterday after our trip to Murano.

Liam headed inside and I took a moment to check my phone; there had been no new messages from Rob which I was thankful for. There *had* been a few messages from Laura, asking how my trip had been so far. I was guilt ridden as I lied about how it was nice to spend time alone, all while trying not to think about what Liam and I had been up to.

I decided to bury my phone in the bottom of my bag and promised myself not to think about home until my feet were firmly on UK soil.

Liam soon returned with a cup of coffee and an iced tea which he placed in front of me.

"Thank you."

"They're going to bring our food out to us when it's ready and then, once we've eaten, I have something planned."

"Which is?" I questioned. "Don't even try to be mysterious, just tell me."

"One of the most cheesy, sappy things you could do in Venice." He shrugged and I urged him on. "I thought we could go on a gondola."

My heart melted; it was something that had been on my list. I hadn't shut up about it to Rob since the holiday was booked.

"Does that sound okay?" Suddenly, he wasn't so sure of his choice, nerves were written all over him.

"No. It sounds perfect." I put my hand over my heart. "Thank you. It was something I wanted to do but it's pretty..." I trailed off.

"Romantic," Liam finished. "If it's too much, tell me. I know we agreed that we're gonna be us while we're in Venice but, if this is too far, then please tell me and I'll find something else."

I reached over the table, grabbing his wrist; he immediately curled his fingers around mine. "Liam, it's perfect and I can't wait," I told him.

One of the waiters then came out with our food and we started to eat, our conversation turning towards our favourite movies and, from there, the rise and fall of the dystopian era.

"*Hunger Games* was far better than *Divergent*."

I shook my head. "See, that is only because it didn't follow the books and let the movies flop."

"You read the books?" I raised my brow.

"Why do you sound so surprised?" He chuckled.

"I don't know actually. I guess I just never thought about you being a reader."

"Well, you should see my room. I have a whole nerdy bookshelf; it's my secret life."

Thing was, I wasn't going to see it because, the second we touched down, we had to go back to being strangers. Which was only hurting more and more with every second I was spending with him.

Liam noticed how quiet I had gone and finished his coffee in one gulp.

"Come on, let's go," he said. "It's just a couple of streets away."

He held out his hand for me again. I took one last sip of my iced tea and took it, whilst swiping my bag off the table. I intertwined my fingers with his as he pulled me onto the path.

It was only a few minutes walk to the gondola stop, except our walk wasn't filled with an awkward silence like our previous ones had been the day before.

My mouth dropped open when I saw the sign spelling out the prices of the ride. Ninety euros per person. It seemed like an insane amount of money to spend on a boat ride.

"Liam, that's one-hundred-and-eighty euros between us." I pulled him to a stop by his bicep before we could get any closer.

"And this is a trip of a lifetime. I have enough saved. Memories are priceless and, if this is all we have, let's make the best ones we can."

I thought about it for a moment; knowing he was right, I nodded. We walked towards the gondolier waiting by the steps. Taking out my phone to snap some pictures, I managed to avoid looking at my notifications. Liam paid for the ride and then called my name.

The middle-aged Italian man smiled at me as I stepped closer, holding out his hand from inside the boat. He was dressed in black trousers, with a white and black striped top. I'd spotted others around the city in a red version or even in plain everyday clothing. Liam was right behind me and I could feel his hand hovering over my waist, ready to catch me if I fell.

I took the gondolier's hand and stepped into the boat.

"You are a sweet couple," he said to me and I didn't deny it this time.

"Thank you." I sat down on the small bench inside the boat as Liam climbed in, rocking it a little. I gripped the edge of my seat, a sea of nerves flooding me as he sat down.

"You okay?" he checked.

"Yeah, I just didn't like the wobbling." I swallowed.

"I got you." He reached out and brushed my knee as the gondolier stepped into position and used the ore to take us away from the side.

Once we were centered in the middle of the canal, slowly moving along, it was easy to lose yourself in the peace of hearing the water. There was the familiar shutter of a camera and I turned to look at Liam, who was pointing his phone right at me.

"You're breaking the rules again," I told him.

"I think the rules are way past broken. No one is going to see. I just think you look beautiful."

"You promise?"

"I have no one worth showing but you really do look beautiful, Es." He turned the camera around, showing me the picture he had taken. I was looking off to the side; even though you couldn't see my eyes, I could tell how at peace I was at.

However, I did feel a little awkward with the gondolier rowing us and not saying anything. I could tell Liam felt the same because he was mostly keeping quiet too. Perhaps that was the beauty of it. There wasn't any need for us to speak. The silence with Liam was nothing like what silence with Rob felt, as if I had done something wrong or I had to calculate what I needed to say to make sure he was happy.

Liam noticed that I was looking at him and offered me a boyish smile, which only made me give him one in return. It was easier to push the guilt of breaking girl code when he looked at me the way he did.

chapter sixteen

A perfect day came to mind. We pulled into the dock and the gondolier tied up the boat. He was smiling at us as he offered me a hand to get out.

"Grazie," I spoke and accepted the help. I stepped back onto the steps and up onto the street again, turning around to see Liam step out and thank him as well, slipping him a ten euro tip.

My lips curled up into a small smile. Liam was kinder than any guy I had come across before, including my ex-boyfriend.

He joined me on the path and I took his hand, waving goodbye to the gondolier as we walked away.

"Did you enjoy it?" Liam asked.

"Every second. Although, don't you feel a little strange when everyone was taking photos and staring at us while we were on the canal, just before we turned into the dock?"

"I guess it's the novelty of them. Or the fact you look like a supermodel." Liam lifted my arm and twirled me around.

I giggled at him as I was turned back in, pressing against him. I placed my hands on his chest and leaned up to kiss him, finding comfort in his lips.

"You're always trying to make me blush," I spoke and Liam lifted a hand to stroke my hair.

"Because you look cute when you're blushing." When he kissed the top of my head, my cheeks were red and I buried my face against his shirt. "Don't hide." I lifted my head. "You don't have to hide with me, Es."

"And you don't have to hide with me either, you can trust me. I know I'm Laura's friend but I'm yours too." There was a twinge of pain as I had to call him a friend, a pain I could see in his eyes as well.

"I know, I'm glad you're here." He kissed the top of my head softly, his lips warm.

"What else do you have planned for today?" I cleared my throat.

"Well, I know how much you love chocolate and I never got round to sharing mine with you last night, so I found a cafe where their hot chocolates are basically melted chocolate. I thought we could go there. And do a little shopping?"

"Good idea. Except for Mom, I haven't got a present for anyone else."

"Let's go, then. " Liam took my hand again and we swung them together as we carried on walking.

"Thank you for today," I told him. "It's been amazing already, I can't thank you enough."

"You don't need to thank me."

My phone ringing was like a cold chill that set over us, along with a great big storm cloud, the kind that would lash down on you and soak you down to the bone. There was a chance that it wasn't Laura or Rob but I still felt sick to my stomach as I pulled my phone from my bag.

It settled slightly once I saw Zoe's face and her caller ID. I answered it, putting my phone to my ear.

"Hey, Zo!"

"Thank god you're alive. I was starting to think you'd been kidnapped or you'd been swept away by a hot Italian."

I took a look at Liam: not Italian but *definitely* hot.

"No, just been enjoying the sights, taking everything in and letting go of what happened back home. How is it at work?"

"Okay, though, Sammy isn't pulling her weight; doing shifts with her is ridiculous and Danny is the shittest manager for making her my cover while you're away. I mean, Sammy, really? She thinks vodka and coke is a cocktail."

"I'll be back in a few days. You can come round when I'm home."

"Oh, my mom asked if you could bring her back some fancy wine to impress her bingo club with."

"Tell Momma Emma I will get her some fancy wine."

"So, what are you going to do for the rest of the day?"

"Just going to do some shopping, get some lunch at a cafe. How about I video call you later and show you the view?"

"Oh my god, yes. I should have just come with you instead of you being on your own."

I swallowed, hating that I was lying to her. "I'm okay, it's been good for me. Honest."

"Okay, well I love you and I'll talk to you later."

"Bye, love you." I hung up the phone, placing it back in my bag. "Sorry, that was Zoe."

"That's the girl with the purple hair, right? You work with her?" Liam questioned, pulling me closer to help me avoid a couple that were just heading straight for us.

"Well, it's blue right now but yeah, that's Zoe. I kind of expected to be getting a call from prison because she'd killed Rob," I joked.

"I wouldn't blame her. She's your best friend and you're hurt."

"Does that mean some of your boys want to kill Laura?" I asked. The concept that she had cheated on Liam was still lost on me.

"No, that would be my little sister, Hanna. She threatened to come home from uni to 'sort her out'." He pointed out a cafe a few doors down. "There it is."

"This looks so cute."

The one he had found had a white exterior which was different to a majority of the old buildings. There were only a couple of tables set out and they were already being used, so we headed straight inside where the white walls carried on but it looked like something out of a palace. A young girl with an apron approached us as soon as we stepped in and welcomed us.

"Hi, could we get a table for two please?" Liam smiled.

"Of course, please follow me."

We were placed right by the window, so we could at least watch the people passing us by. The tables were dressed in soft, white tablecloths with gold embroidery and there were glasses placed on top, next to a small vase of fake roses. Our waitress set two menus in front of us, then walked away.

I took another moment to look around and sighed, completely relaxed. My eyes went back to Liam and a smile crept onto my lips.

"I wish we could stay here forever," I said, without really meaning to.

Liam looked me in the eye. "Believe me, I wish we could too."

"I could totally find a bar to work in. I don't think there are really any golf clubs here."

"Yeah, same here. I'd try and get a manager's job at a bar or restaurant or maybe even open my own."

"Is that something you want to do back home?" I asked, picking up the menu.

"Old Craig, the owner of the pub I work at, is getting older. He's giving me more and more responsibility, so potentially I could be running it by the end of the year. I have savings, almost enough for the mortgage to take it off his hands, so who knows?" He shrugged.

"I think you'd be good at that," I told him. "You have the charisma for it. I've seen you on quiz night."

"I'm the best quiz master, aren't I?" He smirked.

"Ah, there's the ego," I joked. "What are you going to have?"

"The hot chocolate and maybe... the croissant. What about you?"

"The hot chocolate, of course, because that's what we're here for, and the cinnamon roll?"

"That does sound good."

"I tell you what, maybe we can split them and share?" I put down my menu and placed my hands on the table.

Liam nodded. "Yeah, I like that idea. Let's do it."

The waitress came back over to our table and we ordered our drinks and pastries. It was only a few minutes later that she placed two steaming tea cups that looked like they contained pure, melted chocolate.

"Grazie." We both thanked her and she smiled, before walking away.

Liam and I picked up our knives, cutting in half the pastries we had ordered. I picked up part of the cinnamon and placed it on his plate, Liam doing the same with his croissant.

I lifted the hot chocolate to my mouth to take a small sip. Already, it was the perfect temperature to drink and didn't burn my tongue. I'd never tasted anything like it in my life; it was the best chocolate that had ever touched my lips and I moaned.

Liam perked up and, like usual, my cheeks turned as red as strawberries.

"Always blushing and there is no need. Although, I did like that sound coming from you."

"Liam, stop," I whined, laughing and covering my face.

"I can't help it."

"I'd shut up if you want another round before we go out for dinner tonight." I leaned back in my seat with a teasing smirk on my lips.

Liam zipped his mouth shut using his fingers and pretended to throw away the key.

I rolled my eyes but couldn't help but laugh at him, shaking my head.

chapter seventeen

Now that he was in a different room to me, I really did want him back. However, I was standing in the doorway, resting my head on the frame like I was being dropped off at home after a date.

"How long do you need to get ready?" he asked.

"An hour?"

"I'll see you in two."

"Hey!" I gave him a playful shove, the bag of clothes in my hand shaking. "I will see you in an *hour*." I glared, stepping back and closing my door.

I was determined to get ready within the time I promised, just to prove a point. Luckily, I had washed my hair in the morning which meant I was already ahead of schedule. Wiping off my old makeup, I sat in front of the mirror to start again.

I didn't think that it would take long but, before I knew it, I only had ten minutes left; turns out eyeshadow took a lot longer than I thought it did, though it might have just been my attempt to put my eyelashes on that took up most of the time. It was the most makeup I'd worn in the entire trip but I had a smile on my face because of how good I felt.

With only a handful of minutes left, I half pulled my hair back from my face and used a small bobble to hold it there. I left out a few stray ends to frame my face, then dug around my makeup bag for my red lipstick.

Once I'd applied a layer, I pulled my new dress that I'd found in a shop while we were out. It was made from soft black cotton, with a plunging black neckline and splits to reveal both of my legs. The straps were a thick silver chain that lay flat on the front. There was no chance of wearing a bra with it.

In record time, I'd managed to tape up my boobs to give them a lift and slip on my dress. Liam knocked on the door and I reached over to let him in.

"Look, see; I just need to put my shoes on," I spoke, grabbing my black strappy heels.

"I'm impressed. We'll call it sixty-one minutes then, shall we?" He laughed which came to a stand still when he finally looked at me.

I stood in front of him, shoes dangling in my hand, but he was in awe. His face was a picture, blank and speechless.

His hand reached to brush his curls back, the white shirt hugging his muscles as he did so which was hard to ignore. My eyes trailed down to his tight fitting jeans, reminding me of exactly what had turned my stomach upside down.

"I'm taking that as I look okay?" I sat down on the bed, putting my heels on.

"Esme, you look absolutely stunning." Liam shook his head in disbelief.

Like always, my cheeks turned red, though I hoped that my makeup covered it.

"Thank you. This dress was a steal; I don't know how it's going to fit in my case but I'll make it happen," I said, strapping up my heels.

"I was thinking, it's only six, so do you want to go next door for an Aperol spritz before dinner?"

"I'd love that." I stood up and grabbed my little shoulder bag with my phone, room key and bank card. "I'm ready. Let's go."

"Sixity-two minutes." Liam smirked and I rolled my eyes, taking his hand and pulling him out of the room. He shut the door behind us.

We took the usual journey downstairs into the lobby and outside to the view of Rialto bridge. Our table from this morning was free and I sat down in the same seat.

"You want a spritz, yeah?" he asked.

I nodded. "Please."

Liam walked inside and I couldn't wipe the smile off my face. Happy came to mind.

I watched the sight in front of me. There was just over an hour until the sun would set but it was already starting to cool down. The changeover for the dinner service was beginning: the decor and table cloths were being swapped and the wine glasses set out.

Both sides of the street were quieter than they had been in the peak of the day but that was because people were probably napping or getting ready for the evening. The smell of the bakeries had settled down and had been replaced with fresh flowers that carried through the breeze, along with the faint smell of fresh pizza too.

Liam walked out with large wine glasses full of golden, orange liquid and ice, putting one in front of me.

"Thank you."

"No problem, gorgeous."

It was the first time he had called me that outside of us sleeping together which made my heart flutter in ways that it shouldn't. But it was the way I knew a girl deserved to be treated, a way I hadn't been treated in a long time.

I picked up my glass and took a sip of my Aperol spritz, nodding in satisfaction.

"Have you enjoyed today?" he asked me.

"Of course I have, it was absolutely perfect. This whole trip has been, even if I didn't expect it to turn out the way it did it. Going home is going to be a shock to the system."

"Maybe it doesn't have to be."

"You know it does. I've broken so many girl code rules just being here." There was the guilt again, ready to swallow me whole.

Liam nodded but he looked sad.

"I want to. I wish I could, Liam. I really do. Because, honestly, you've been more kind to me than anyone has before and I'm seeing you in a completely different light now, after all the time I've spent with you over the past three years."

"I didn't expect things to happen the way they did either. I just knew how you were feeling that night at the bus stop. I didn't want you to suffer the way I had been for the past week. And now I'm sitting here with you and I can't imagine doing this with anyone else in this world."

The truth was that everything Liam was saying to me was the way I felt as well.

We were meant to be here with two people we loved and, in the end, they were the people who had hurt us the most. Laura had done something unimaginable; it was hard to believe she had hurt

Liam the same way Rob had hurt me. We'd come to escape them, escape the pain and upset. It was no wonder that we'd started to fall for each other. At least, that's what I thought was happening.

"You wouldn't think you could start to like someone so quickly after having your heart broken. Most people would say this is just a rebound, for both of us," I spoke. "But I don't think it is. I think it's real, more real than anything I've felt in years, because you care and you treat me well. Whether it's just that you feel sorry for me, I don't know."

"I *don't* feel sorry for you, that's not what I meant. Do you know, this trip is the first time I've laughed properly in a long time?"

"You always seemed so happy before."

"So did you. It's what you do, though, isn't it? When you're unhappy, you fake it, thinking it will make all of it better."

"None of it changes anything. I might like you but I *can't* like you."

"I'd never pressure you into giving this a chance but, if this is all I have with you, then I intend to make it the best time of my life."

"Liam." I sighed.

"Esme."

"This is such a mess." I closed my eyes.

"Tell me about it."

I decided the best thing to do was to pick up my drink and let go of all my senses, before the guilt finished me. It was the same broken record over and over again: the fight and struggle to understand the feelings I was having, along with the loyalty I was supposed to have for my friend. Though, there was also the struggle with the fact she had cheated on Liam and yet was furious that Rob had done that to me.

"We have one more day. Let's just try to enjoy it," I said, taking another swig out of my glass.

chapter eighteen

It was the perfect night and it was the perfect last day. Nothing could have pulled me from my height of happiness, except the plane ticket home that was like a time bomb that neither of us spoke about.

Liam's room had become redundant; he'd stayed with me when we'd returned from dinner and hadn't gone back to it, other than for his things.

Liam was watching me as I brushed my hair, sitting on the bed.

"What?" I asked.

"You really don't know how beautiful you are." He smiled at me. I tried to return it, only mine ended up sad. "What's wrong, gorgeous?" He walked towards me, his body towering over, and I looked up.

"We go home tomorrow."

Liam cupped my cheek, stroking my face, and I relaxed into his touch.

"Then let's make the most of it." He kissed the top of my head and, before another word could leave my lips, I squealed from being picked up. Instinctively, I wrapped my arms around his neck as he took us into the bathroom, sitting me on the counter. All I could think about was the last time we were in the bathroom together and the way he had fucked me while I looked in the mirror.

And now, his hands rested on either side of me as he stood between my thighs.

"You need to relax and I have just the thing. It's avocado." He picked up the tub of face mask that had been an issue at the airport and I giggled, taking it from him.

I unscrewed the lid and picked some of the green mask onto my fingers, swiping it onto his nose.

Liam grinned at me as I decorated his face with the sludge. Once I was done, he wiggled his eyebrows at me.

"Well, how do I look?" he asked.

"Hmmm, bit like shrek." Liam was quick to wipe some of the mask on my own nose. "Hey!"

"Shut up." He planted a hard kiss on my lips and I melted, not caring that I was getting some of the avocado on me. When Liam pulled away, it was hard to not stare into his eyes. I took a moment to take him in for my memory's sake.

Then he picked up the tub and started to paint my skin. I didn't take my eyes off him as he covered each inch of my face.

"Beautiful," he whispered, stealing a peck on my lips. I wasn't sure how I was going to ever let him go.

Our faces were clean and rejuvenated but our legs were sore and there were blisters on our feet; though, it didn't stop us curling up in bed together for the last time. Our bags were packed and Liam had turned on the TV, pretending he could actually understand what was going on. I stared at my cabin case and his duffel in the corner of the room.

"Esme? Are you okay?" Liam reached over the bed and tucked a piece of loose blonde hair behind my ear.

"It's like the last twenty-four hours went so quickly. Like, it was only seconds ago we were bickering at dinner about enjoying our last day and now it's gone." I turned to look him in the eye and, for the first time since we arrived, they were as sad, just like they had been at the bus stop.

I leaned in and pressed my lips against his in a sweet kiss, hoping for some miracle that I could take away the pain, like he had mine on this trip. The kiss was reciprocated and Liam tangled his hand in the waves of my hair. I shuffled closer to him on the bed, making it easier to touch one another. We were sitting up, side by side, my legs bent towards him, as he reached out, wrapping a hand around my thigh, massaging my skin.

"One last time," I whispered against his lips.

"What do you want?" he asked.

"You, slow. I want to feel everything, remember every second."

Make love.

But how could it have been love in just a short amount of time?

Liam maneuvered, laying me down on the bed, sweet and gentle. I looked up at him as he brushed back his hair, before leaning down to press his lips against mine in one of his to-die-for kisses. I didn't want to stop. It was the *last* thing I wanted and my heart ached, knowing that, by the next evening, our trip would be a distant memory.

A tear slipped from my eye and it must have touched Liam because he pulled back.

"If you cry, *I'll* cry." He brushed it away. "Pretend, at least for tonight, that this is forever."

I nodded, forcing back the tears and telling myself that I would cry once I was in the comfort of my own flat again.

I stretched up, my lips against Liam's again and pretended, just like he'd asked. Yet, I still photographed and memorised the way his lips felt against mine and the way his hand slid up my waist. I knew Liam well enough that he was getting harder with every second, without even feeling it pressed against me. Then, when the time was right, he pushed his hips down, so I knew what was coming.

Liam pulled down his shorts, revealing his hard cock that I had come to enjoy so much. His fingers slipped into PJ shorts and took them off. I helped kick them from my ankles, leaving my bottom half bare. Very awkwardly, I slipped off my vest top. I'd taken my bra off as soon as we'd gotten in, so I was completely naked in front of him. Liam quickly got rid of his own top, before opening my thighs enough for him to get close.

A whimper escaped my lips as I felt him slowly push himself inside of me. It was a relief, us being together again.

I was going to feel so lost without him. So, I made sure, in that moment, I took in every second of how he made me feel.

Every thrust was carefully calculated, slow and deep, just as I'd asked. Liam bit down on his bottom lip as he moved, his eyes almost rolling into the back of his head. I'd never felt more sexy in my entire life. It was just nice to feel so wanted, so *loved*.

I wrapped my arms around his neck and tugged him closer so that our lips would touch. I wanted to feel him in every way that I could, gasping when he pushed a little deeper. It was painful but the good kind that only made me wetter.

The sound of my pussy and our heavy breathing was all that I could hear. Liam rocked his hips a little faster, finding a rhythm that suited us both. One of his hands reached up, gently rolling my nipple between his fingers.

I pulled away, my head falling to the side to let out a moan. Liam kissed the side of my neck.

"I wish we could stay here forever." My voice cracked.

"Stay with me, gorgeous," he whispered. "Be here with me right now."

I nodded, closing my eyes, sliding my hand between us to find my clit, my knuckles brushing his stubble as he thrusted inside of me again.

"I'm here," I mumbled, the knot in my stomach starting to build as I rubbed myself in gentle circles.

I opened my eyes, turning to look at him.

"Let me be on top." It wasn't something I did often; being on top made me feel insecure. But, with Liam, that feeling was non-existent. When he pulled out, I missed the warmth and connection of him inside of me.

We moved position. Liam lay his head on the pillows and I moved to get on top, hesitating for a split moment. Liam saw it, there was no way he could *miss* it. He wrapped his hands around my hips and guided me on top of him.

"You okay?" He raised a brow at me.

"I'm okay." I smiled, gliding my wet pussy up and down his hard cock.

"Tease," he hissed, moving one hand to help himself slide inside of me.

I began to rock my hips slowly, trying to find an ounce of confidence.

Liam could see it, *sense* it. Instead of ridiculing me, he helped me, lifting his hips to thrust up inside of me.

The sensation surprised me and I gasped. The longer I was on top, the easier it was to take control. I placed my hands either side of him, lifting my ass up to ride him.

I liked the look in Liam's eyes as I rode him, imagining the bliss in them wasn't much different to my own. Liam gripped my thighs as he struggled to hold back his own moans.

"I want you to cum in me, Liam," I told him. "I want you to fill me."

Liam's eyes were glimmering, biting down on his lip as I slowly teased him, gently pulling myself up to his tip and pushing myself down again. I was battling to hold myself back, wanting to feel every inch of him.

I was close and my hands were shaking as I tethered on the edge of climax. It was only when I could feel Liam's balls tighten under me that I cried out, shattering on top of him, falling onto his chest. My pussy tightened around his cock.

He thrust himself up into me one last time, filling me with his cum. I sighed against the crook of his neck, revelling in the feeling.

When I attempted to lift myself up off him, Liam tensed his grips on my thighs.

"Not yet," he murmured.

Happy to comply, I snuggled closer, our sweaty skin sticking to each other.

"I'm going to miss you," I whispered.

"I'm going to miss you too," he replied, kissing my shoulder.

Another tear managed to escape me.

chapter nineteen

I felt sick as I packed my clothes into the small cabin case I had brought with me, growling to myself as it wouldn't all fit. Why was that always the way? I threw the last pieces in on top and crammed down the lid, trying to slide the zip around. The suitcase and bag were the last thing to do, as Liam had checked us in for our flight after I'd fallen asleep in his arms the night before.

"Here, sit on top." Liam walked towards me.

I perched myself on the case as he stood in front of me, still shirtless; he leaned over to help shut my busting case.

"Thanks," I whispered.

Liam gave me a sad smile and kissed me.

Every last stolen moment that our lips touched reminded me that we were going home.

"We need to stop."

"Yeah, I agree."

Yet it didn't stop me from wrapping my arms around his neck and pulling him closer. The kiss was desperate; we were clawing at one another's clothes and I'm sure they would come off our bodies if we had the time. Liam palmed my tits so well under my dress that I could have asked him to risk taking me quickly but we needed to be at the airport in just under an hour.

Breathless and hot, I squeezed my eyes shut and forced myself to pull away. I placed my hands on his chest, pushing, creating space between us again.

"We *really* need to stop."

Not that we'd slip up at home because there was no reason to see each other again... but it was going to make things a whole lot worse.

Harder to get over.

Harder to move on.

For a moment, I took in Liam for the last time, promising myself that I would start to distance myself for my own good. The morning sun highlighted the edges of his face, making his brown hair look warm and inviting with it tucked behind his ears.

"I hate this." He swallowed.

"Me too." And that was the truth.

The truth hurt.

I slid off the top of my case, dragging it down onto the floor.

There hadn't been an awkward silence for a long time between us but that's all there was as we checked out, paid the visitor's tax and waited outside for the water bus to take us back to the pick up point. There was nothing to say because I didn't know *what* to say, neither of us did. Liam didn't even dare to speak when he helped me pick up my case and put it on the bus.

Paradise was truly over and, as much as I didn't want to, all I could think about was how much I wanted to go back in time, to the start of the trip, to the night we first slept together, and do everything all over again in a loop forever.

But I had to remember Liam wasn't mine.

He was Laura's.

Even though they weren't together anymore.

Though it didn't make me feel any less shit about what I had done while we had been in Venice.

I sat on the wall close to the pick up point, texting Zoe that I was on my way home and she needed to be at mine with a bottle of wine when she had finished work.

Strangely, the black taxi that had brought us into the city was the same one that turned up again to take us back to the airport. The driver helped us place our bags in the boot of the car, then Liam and I slid into the back seat. I attempted to make as much space as I could between us.

I kept my eyes looking outside of the window as we drove, pretending that Liam's aftershave hadn't crawled up my nose and made me think about him.

"You okay?" he asked, which took me by surprise.

I turned my head so that I could catch a glimpse of him. "Yeah, just not looking forward to going back to work." The lie slipped far too easily from my tongue.

"Hmm, my shift at the pub isn't looking too appealing either. Do you think you'll see Rob when you get back?"

I wasn't quite sure why he was asking, perhaps it was jealousy or maybe he was worried about Rob giving me grief. Or... he wanted to look after me.

"No. Not by choice at least. I never gave him his own key to the flat, he didn't want one, so he shouldn't be any bother."

Hindsight is always a wonderful thing; it should have been a massive red flag, the fact he didn't even want to commit and move into the flat with me. That was only the *first* red flag.

By the time we had reached the airport, I'd gone through every inch of my relationship with Rob, how I should have escaped before he had managed to hurt me. Found someone like Liam instead.

Liam helped me with my suitcase and I thanked him. Luckily, he had transferred my boarding pass onto my phone so I didn't have to wait for him; I made my way into the airport on my own.

"Esme! Esme, wait up!" I could hear him calling for me, guilt washing over me.

I took a deep breath and stopped in my tracks, twirling on my heel to watch him rushing to catch up with me.

"Come on, don't act like we're strangers;, it's not going to help either of us."

"I'm just trying to get back to normal. Holiday is over."

"We haven't left Venice yet." He reached for my hand. "So, until we've touched down on the ground in Birmingham, then you can at least pretend you still like me."

It wasn't pretend.

I wanted to tell him.

And I wished we could have stayed in Venice forever, like we had talked about that one time.

"Okay." I swallowed and hoped that he didn't kiss me because it would break me at this point. Instead, we linked our fingers together and started to walk, hand in hand.

One last time.

The airport was already busy for mid-morning and we headed straight for security thanks to the ease of internet check in. We stood in line, waiting to go through the scanners and our bags to be put through security.

"What's the first thing you're going to do when you get home?" Liam asked, still holding my hand.

Tilting my head, I considered what exactly I was going to do. "Buy fresh bread, make some toast and wait for Zoe to come around with a bottle of wine."

"Make some toast?" He laughed. "I thought you'd be doing something a little more exciting than that."

"I might even put a load of washing on." I swung our hands.

"Oh, you rebel," he teased me.

I wanted to laugh and smile with him but, instead, I began slowly building the wall. To protect me and to protect him, no one else needed to be hurt in this situation. Especially Liam and I, not when we had just started to heal.

"I fancy an iced coffee," I said, pointing out the small Starbucks kiosk in the corner of duty free.

"Caramel latte?" he asked.

I shook my head. "Iced caramel macchiato, please."

The smile Liam gave me was almost sad and there was a twinge in my heart. I wanted to throw away the tickets and passports and make the dream we talked about that night come true. I wasn't a hundred percent sure if Liam would even follow me, although it seemed like he had been struggling the most with the fact we needed to stop kissing, stop everything.

I couldn't take my eyes off him as he stood in the queue for our coffees. But then, my phone went off and I pulled it from my bag; Zoe had texted me, wishing me a safe flight, and telling me that she'd be there when I got home. I couldn't have been more grateful.

My finger hovered over my chat with Laura that had been quiet since our call. The guilt swayed over me and I pushed it to the bottom of my stomach as I put my phone back in my bag. Tightening my knuckles around the handle of my little suitcase, I thought about how I'd have to keep Liam and our time together locked away in a little box. He would just be a story I told my grandchildren in the future. The guy who healed my heart when I didn't see a way out of the black pit it had been left in.

I plastered a fake smile on my face as he approached, with two coffees and a couple of paper bags. He passed me my drink, then one of the bags.

"I got you an almond croissant as well. It's probably not the same as the bakery yesterday but still, one last taste of Venice."

"Thank you." He was still being so kind. But, there was an undertone I hadn't heard before, one that just seemed so familiar.

Sadness.

Just like mine.

"I'm not sure if the gate will be on the board yet, so I suggest we-"

"Shop." I finished for him and Liam groaned.

"I thought you'd be done shopping by now."

"Not at all, come on." As I turned towards the duty free shopping, my suitcase was pulled from my hand.

"I got it. Come on."

The smile on my face went from fake to real. I started to realise that I was going to miss him a whole lot more than I thought I was going to. My attempt to distract myself was futile, though. I couldn't help taking a glance at him a second too long everytime he wasn't looking. When he caught me, I'd just carry on nibbling on my croissant, feigning my innocence.

My other way of coping was spending all the money I had left on three bottles of perfume, a tub of pringles and more Kinder chocolate than anyone possibly needed; I started eating it while we were in the line for passport control and our boarding line.

I passed over my documents to the woman who was scanning them. From the moment she looked at us, I knew what was going to come out of her mouth.

"Romantic trip? Bet you're both upset it's over?"

Only this time, it was Liam that spoke up. "No, no. We're just friends." It sounded like he was swallowing nails.

The check-in assistant blushed out of embarrassment. "Sorry about that. Umm, enjoy your flight."

I took my passport from her and my suitcase from Liam.

"No worries. Honestly."

Liam and I made our way down the corridor. The holiday blues were starting to set in as we walked out into the open and followed the cones towards the plane. We walked side by side the whole way there and he only stepped aside to let me go up the steps first.

I greeted the cabin workers standing by the door and headed to find our row without even looking back. But, before I could lift my case into the overhead cabin, Liam was there, doing it for me.

"Thank you." I slipped into the window seat as he shoved his duffel bag above and sat next to me. I compressed my legs together as much as I could so we didn't touch. Pulling out my AirPods and power bank, I shoved them into the netted pocket, then put my bag under the seat in front of me. Liam did the same and slouched into his seat, putting his hood over his head.

I turned away, looking outside the window while everyone else boarded.

Neither of us spoke a word as they all took their seats.

No one sat next to our aisle seat.

The last time we were going to be alone.

As soon as the plane was in the sky, I carried on watching *The Vampire Diaries* like I had on the way to Venice, distracting myself from the fact we were up in the air.

I was content, sipping on my can of Sprite and watching my show, until the turbulence hit. It almost took my breath away as the plane rattled and the moment of panic flooded my body. Liam perked up from watching his own phone and grabbed my hand.

"Hey, you're okay. It'll pass," he spoke, pulling an AirPod from his ear.

The Captain's announcement came from the speaker. But it didn't matter. My mind couldn't concentrate on anything as the plane jolted again.

"You're okay. Cap said it'll pass in a few moments."

I gripped onto his forearms as the plane shook again.

"Fucking hell. This is it, isn't it?" I swallowed.

Liam laughed at me and squeezed his hand.

"Well, if we're going to die, what about one last kiss?"

I glared.

"I'm kidding! I'm trying to distract you."

The plane rattled again, only lighter this time.

"I was really enjoying *The Vampire Diaries*."

"Yeah, where were you at? Season two was always my favourite."

"You've watched it?" I loosened my grip as Liam smiled at me. "First part of season two was my favourite. I was gutted when Katherine got locked up in the tomb."

"Ah, Katherina Petrova. Queen of Hell."

"I always knew she hadn't been sucked into oblivion."

"I also liked Elijah; he was the best original. Did you watch the spin off?"

"Yeah, it was really good. It was a shame they cancelled it."

"Favourite character?" he asked.

"Davina or Hayley."

"And have you noticed the plane has stopped shaking?"

I looked around, noticing that everyone else had settled back down. And then I turned back. Liam smiled at me and I wanted to kiss him again, thank him for talking me through the turbulence.

Though it was more than a thought because, before I knew it, we were inching closer and closer. Our lips almost touched but I turned my head away.

"We can't."

"I know..."

chapter twenty

There's always that moment in the rom-com where the two people that had fallen in love look back when they were leaving one another. Not that I had fallen in love with Liam. I *couldn't* have. But we did have that moment as we parted ways. My taxi was waiting for me and he had gone towards the shuttle to collect his car.

It only lasted for a split second but it felt like forever.

A montage of our holiday together played in my head and I wished that we could have stayed there forever, like we had planned. Anything was better than standing at Birmingham Airport and making each other into strangers.

Liam brushed his curls back from his head and turned away from me.

"Goodbye," I whispered to myself as I walked away from all the beautiful times we had shared while in Venice.

Approaching the small row of taxis waiting in the rink, I saw one with my name on the windscreen. I lifted my hand to the driver and he climbed out of the cab to help me.

"Afternoon, my lovely. How was your holiday?" he asked, taking my case from me and lifting it into the cab.

"Good, thank you." I had the feeling that my trip home wasn't going to be in solitude.

"Where are you coming from?"

"Venice, just a few days." I spoke, climbing into the back. The driver shut the door behind me and sat back into his seat.

"On your own?"

"With… a friend." I swallowed. I wasn't quite sure I could even call Liam a friend anymore; we'd blurred that line before we could even finish drawing it.

"Me and the missus went to Venice back in the day, though it's far more of a tourist destination…" Then there was no stopping him the entire way home. The more he spoke of how romantic it was and how much he loved his wife, the more depressed I felt to be back in the UK.

I tried to zone out, watching the grey and dull streets, which didn't help my mood in the slightest. Pulling up outside of my dingy little studio flat, I sighed. Home sweet home, I guess.

"Keep the change." I smiled, reaching between the front seats to hand him a twenty pound note.

"No problem, my dear. Have a great day."

"Thank you." I got out of the cab and grabbed my suitcase, shutting the door behind me and heading to the entrance of my building. Luckily, there was one floor between me and my comfy bed. My very lonely bed.

I fought with my keys in the bottom of my bag as I approached my front door, before unlocking it for the first time in what felt like ages. The smell of home comforts hit, fading Marc Jacobs perfume and fresh bed sheets I'd put on before I'd left.

I pushed the suitcase to the side and closed the door. Sitting on my small corner kitchen countertop was a bag for life.

My things from Rob's were there and a note. It read: *Got your stuff back, love Laura.* I scrunched the note up and threw it in the bin.

The moment my body hit the sofa was the greatest relief of my life as I curled up and lay my head on the crochet pillow that my mom had made me when I was little.

The silence was deafening.

Having Liam for company had almost been enough to stop me thinking or change them so they were all about him.

I tugged down the blanket on the back of the sofa and reached for the TV remote, telling myself that my washing could wait. But, before I could even turn it on, my phone rang. Huffing, I stood and went over to my bag to answer the call.

"Hey, Zo." I switched the call to speaker and walked back towards the sofa.

"I am so happy you're home. So, I'm about fifteen minutes away. I have three bottles of wine and thought we could order a curry. I know you're probably sick of eating pizza and pasta."

"Sounds perfect. I think I have some ice cream in the freezer too. Oh, do you think you could grab me some milk and bread if you pass a shop, please?"

"Already got you some. I'll see you soon."

"Thanks, Zo. Love ya." We hung up and I opened my texts to Laura. I had to start getting back to normal, even though I was going to be riddled with guilt for the rest of my life. I sent a text asking if she wanted to join me and Zoe, then put my phone down.

There was no point trying to watch anything, not with Zoe on her way, so I decided that I should do a load of washing and get back to normality. I sat on my floor, sorting my dirty clothes into whites, blacks and colours, picking whites to go on first with the old sheets from my washing basket. By the time I clicked 'go' on my machine, Zoe knocked on my door.

She wrapped her arms around me the moment that I let her in, the bag of wine rattling and the loaf of bread whacking me in the back as I hugged her back.

"How was it? Meet any hot Italian men?" she joked, pulling back. My jaw dropped as I spotted her bright pink hair.

"When did you do that?" I tugged on a strand.

"I got bored last night. The blue was a real bitch but now my hair feels like straw." She sighed, walking over to my counter to put everything down.

"I don't know how it hasn't fallen out." I reached for the wine glasses in my cupboard and passed them to her.

"Anyway, hot Italians?"

There were three options in that moment. I could lie and tell her that I didn't meet anyone, lie and pretend Liam had been a holiday romance which wasn't necessarily a complete lie or tell her the truth and risk Zoe thinking I was a complete and utter slut.

"Yeah, about that... I'd pour yourself a glass." I cleared my throat.

Zoe raised her eyebrow as she cracked open the first bottle of Blossom Hill.

"And you have to promise not to think bad of me because I already think bad of myself."

"Dear lord, please don't tell me you took back that cheating bastard?" She began pouring wine into our glasses.

"No but it breaks so many girl rules. I feel like complete shit." My eyes began to water now that I was saying it out loud.

Zoe's curiosity turned into concern and she frowned, passing me some wine.

I took a large swig before I spoke again. "I wasn't on my own. I went with Liam."

Zoe blinked twice. "Laura's boyfriend?"

"Laura's *ex*. They broke up a while back. She cheated on him. And, the day I found out about Rob, I saw Liam at the bus stop and he said they'd broken up. He said that he was still going on the trip to Venice and asked if I wanted to get away. Just as friends." My next large swig must have given me away.

"You didn't stay 'just friends', did you?" she asked.

A tear rolled down my cheek, confirming her suspicions.

"I'm such a shit friend and it's not like I did anything really wrong. They aren't together anymore but-"

"Girl code. So, you feel like crap." She leaned against the counter as I picked up the bottle to top up my glass. "Hang on, though. Why didn't Laura say anything?"

"Maybe she was ashamed? Especially after what Rob had done to me. I never thought she would cheat on Liam but I don't know what she did or who with."

"Fuck." Zoe shook her head.

"God, I'm such an awful person. How am I even meant to look her in the eye ever again? We were drunk. At least, we were the *first* time. It was just sex. But then, fuck things got messy."

"Oh girlie, have you got feelings for him?"

I necked half of my glass. "It's probably just trauma bonding," I lied. It was more than that. It was the kind of crush that came crashing down with no warning, from something I expected after having my heart broken.

"And if it's not?"

"It *has* to be. It's not like I'm ever going to see him again. The trip is over and he's broken up with Laura. What happened in Venice is staying there. Laura can't know."

"Yeah, agreed. I mean, I can't believe she cheated on Liam and then slagged Rob off like that."

"Maybe there was something else going on with her. Not like I can ask her; she'll need to tell me first, else she'll know I've spoken to Liam."

"I don't think wine was the right choice. Vodka would have been better."

I nodded, taking a sip this time. "Yeah." I wiped the tear from my cheek with the back of my hand.

"Oh, Esme. Please don't get yourself upset. You can't help feelings and you sure as hell can't help a drunken mistake. You were both single. It's okay." Zoe put down her glass and wrapped her arms around me again as I wept into her shoulder.

"I don't even know why I'm crying."

"You've been through a lot this past month; no one can blame you for any of it. Come on, let's sit down, find some crappy romance movie on the TV and order a curry."

"First, I really want a piece of toast." I began to open the bread and Zoe laughed at me.

Telling someone had helped the guilt a little but I still struggled with what Laura would think if she knew what had developed between Liam and I. For a moment, I could almost forget what had happened in Venice and let everything go back to normal. At least, up until I got a text from Liam.

Just got home from the pub with the boys. Hope you got home safe.

Something innocent, not even suggestive, just kind.

chapter twenty-one

Normality had resumed. I'd been home for two days and I'd started back at work, Liam's text still left unreplied to. I spent every waking moment trying to ignore that fact.

With a few hours left until I needed to get to work, I'd decided to hang out with my mom. Part of me missed being back home and going back was always comforting.

I pushed down the porch door handle and kicked off my shoes inside, before letting myself into the house.

"Hello?" I called.

"In the kitchen, darling."

Walking in, I saw Mom standing at the hob, stirring one of her sage green pans. I propped myself against the opposite counter and put my tote bag on the side too.

"I'm just warming up some chilli for lunch. Have you eaten?" She glanced over her shoulder.

"Yeah, I had some cheese on toast not long ago." I smiled.

Mom turned off the stove, turning around to pull me into a hug. "I'm so glad you're back. You're glowing. That trip really made a world of difference, didn't it?"

"Yeah, something like that." I rubbed her back, then pulled away to reach for my bag, taking out her present. "Here, I got you this." I passed it to her and she cooed.

"Oh, darling, you didn't have to get me anything!" she spoke while unwrapping it like a kid at Christmas.

The Murano glass sparkled under the sun, shining through the back door.

Looking at the figure only reminded me of that day...

The way Liam and I almost kissed inside the shop, only to actually kiss when I'd ran away.

On reflection, it was that day that had really started to blur the lines, nevermind the night before. That entire day had been perfect; I'd started to see Liam as a person, rather than my friend's ex.

I debated on telling my mom what had happened, perhaps ask for some advice. But the fear took over me and I didn't have a bottle of wine to catch my fall, like I had with Zoe.

"Earth to Esme. What's gotten into you, darling?"

I shrugged.

"Nothing, I was just thinking about how beautiful it was. There were what felt like hundreds of shops where people were making all these gorgeous pieces of glass art. There was nothing like it. It was almost magical..." I rambled, leaving out every mention of Liam.

"I'm glad you enjoyed yourself. It's just what you needed. I was telling the girls at the cafe about that slimy little Rob and, well, all I'll say is he best not come in for a while, else he might find a few surprises in his breakfast." She put the glass gondola on the windowsill with a few other trinkets from various holidays she had been on.

"They don't need to do that." I shook my head. "I'm okay, honestly. I'm moving forward with my life. I was never going to be able to do that with Rob."

Mom cupped my face and it was a struggle to hold back the tears. There was something about your mom giving you comfort that broke all defences.

"You deserve more than him. You deserve a man who listens to your dreams, wants to dream *with* you. One that whisks you away to magical places, just like Venice."

Little did she know I had found someone who had done just that. He just couldn't be mine.

"Now, no more of those tears... Would you like a brew?" She tapped my cheek.

"I would love one." I forced a smile onto my face.

A fresh cup of tea almost made things okay but it didn't make me want to head to work. The lack of traffic meant I ended up sitting in the car park, in the same place I'd been after I found out what Rob had done. My face started to burn. All those feelings started to surface and I rested my forehead on the steering wheel.

"No, Esme," I whispered to myself. "Distract yourself."

My distraction was only worse: looking at the text that Liam had sent. There hadn't been another and he probably hated me for not replying in the first place but, slowly, I began to write out a reply.

Hey, sorry I haven't been in touch. Things have been crazy. Just heading to work for my first shift back.

I pretty much threw my phone into my open bag on the passenger seat, as if it was radioactive.

Sending texts was not 'keeping it in Venice'.

I grabbed my tote bag and climbed out of the car with a sigh.

"Hello, Esme!"

I looked over the car park to see one of the golden girls from the country club.

"Hiya, Annie. I hope you've had a good day." I waved.

"And you, my doll. I've left a drink behind the bar for you. Take care, sweetie." She was the golden girl that treated all the staff like they were her grandchildren to be exact.

I walked into the bar and noticed that Zoe hadn't arrived yet, seeing Sammy behind the bar struggling to make a cosmo.

"God help," I muttered.

I dumped my bag in the staff room and walked behind the bar. Sammy glanced at me sideways.

"Hey." I offered an awkward smile.

"Hi. Zoe is late. So, I'm glad you're here. I'm clocking off. That's for Mrs Clapham." She poured her watery cosmo into the glass, then pulled off her tabard.

As soon as she was out of sight, I tipped her cosmo down the sink and remade it. The thought of my reputation being poured down the drain because of a shit cocktail was not on my list.

Twenty minutes later, Zoe rushed in, her cheeks flushed.

"Es, I am so, so sorry. My mom... she fell down the stairs, again. I had to take her to A&E and then she wouldn't let me leave."

"Don't worry about it. Sammy, on the other hand... Oh, she's gonna lock you in the kitchen freezer or waterboard you with watery cosmos. Why does she add *water*?"

"She thinks there's too much alcohol. I give up and just remake them, at least until the customer is drunk."

"We need to tell Danny again," I said, grabbing a fresh bottle of orange juice for the shot of vodka sitting on the side.

"I'm pretty sure they are doing it in the staff room," Zoe whispered in my ear.

"What?!" My jaw dropped.

Zoe nodded, throwing her pink hair up in a ponytail.

"I'm going to give this to table six and then I want all the details."

"I got you." She smiled.

Normality was key.

chapter twenty-two

Shifts were better when you had good company and I loved the ones I had with Zoe, especially when we stole the last slices of chocolate cake from the kitchen. After all, waste not want not.

I waved to her as she closed the door of my car.

"Love you," she called, dashing into her house.

"Love you too."

Driving back to my studio only took me ten minutes and the closer I got, the more excited I was to kick off my shoes and lay in bed. Once I'd parked my car, I yawned on cue, reaching for my tote bag and getting out.

I wasn't paying much attention as I walked up the steps to my floor. It wasn't until I looked up to put my key in the door that I noticed Liam standing there. Three Dominos boxes were in his hand and a bottle of wine was under his arm. I was frozen still.

He offered a small, awkward smile.

"What are you doing here?" I raised an eyebrow at him.

"You didn't reply to my text. And, well I was missing Venice. The pizza isn't as good but it's pizza."

"We promised what happened between us was going to stay in Venice." I swallowed, unlocking my door.

"We both know that we weren't going to keep that promise."

"Liam."

"Esme."

My mind was at a crossroads: I could turn him away or I could invite him inside and do something selfish that could end up with me losing Laura. Yet, how much did she actually care about him if she'd been cheating on him? I sighed and pushed open the door.

"Get in," I told him.

A small smile danced on his lips as he walked into my humble abode.

"It's not a lot. It was only meant to be a stop gap until I move out with Rob but looks like I'm going to be stuck here a little bit longer."

I watched Liam look around my dinky studio flat.

"It's lovely, don't knock yourself down. I mean, I still live with my parents so you've accomplished more than me. Where do you want to eat?"

"The coffee table is okay," I said, kicking off my shoes. "I'm just going to get changed."

Walking over to my drawers, I began to stress that I only had *My Little Pony* or Disney PJs that were clean and not in the slightest bit attractive. Which was not something I should have even been thinking about. I pulled open the third drawer and was glad to be greeted by my pink and heart PJ set, taking it out in relief. I turned to look at Liam, who was sitting on the edge of my sofa with the coffee table full of food in front of him.

"I'm just going to get changed and I'll grab a couple of glasses."

Once I'd shut myself inside of the bathroom, I pushed my body against the door and took a deep breath.

"Esme, what the fuck are you doing?" I whispered to myself, squeezing my eyes shut. Him being in my flat was only going to make the feelings that I had grown for him stronger. If he was planning on sticking around, then there was no chance that I was going to be able to stop the feelings from growing or snuff them out completely.

I shook my head and began to strip down to get changed, leaving on my bra for some bizarre reason, as if he hadn't seen me without one before. Checking my hair in the mirror, I pulled it back into a fresh bun and cleaned the smudged mascara under my eyes. At the last second, I decided to use mouthwash, even though I was about to eat pizza.

When I opened the bathroom door, Liam had made himself a little more comfortable and was sitting back, scrolling on his phone. The pizza had been left untouched on the coffel table, waiting for me to sit down too. Thanks to my two seater sofa, we would be sitting way too close to each other for my liking. One touch and I was likely to crumble.

I grabbed two glasses from the cupboard and then sat next to him, trying to keep myself curled up as possible.

"So, what do we have?" I asked.

Liam put down his phone and flipped open the pizza box. "Half ham and pineapple, the other side peperoni with olives."

My heart could have imploded in that moment. Something so simple as olives... but he had *remembered*. That was what meant the world to me.

"You got me olives?" My voice cracked in awe.

"Well, we all have our guilty pleasures. " Liam shrugged and, for once, he blushed. "I also got chicken strips, wedges combo and four cookies."

I reached over and put the glasses down, watching Liam crack open the bottle of white wine he had bought with him. He poured half a glass, then passed it to me.

"Thanks." I took a sip; it was nice but nothing like Venice.

"Want to watch a movie or something while we eat?" he asked.

I shook my head.

"Nah, we can just talk. There was no TV at dinner in Venice. Besides, I haven't scolded you enough for just turning up here." I pursed my lips.

"I missed Venice. I missed *you*." He looked away and picked up a slice. "As a friend, obviously."

"Liar," I spilled out. If I was lying, then he was as well. That or I was going to have the most embarrassing moment of my life.

"Says the one so determined for everything to stay in Venice that she's locked herself away and won't even let me back."

" You're still my friend's ex," I spoke.

"She broke my heart, Esme."

"So, going after her best friend is what? Payback?" I put my glass on the table and crossed my arms.

"Esme. Come on, it's not like that at all. I didn't expect things to happen the way they did. I'd never even considered that me and you would even work til Venice. I asked you to come on that trip because you were hurting, hurting just like I was. I couldn't make myself feel better and I wanted to do something. Yeah, you happened to be there and I knew exactly how you were feeling. I thought going to Venice would put a smile on your face again."

"I feel like I've cheated, just like *he* did, betrayed my best friend."

"This isn't some twisted game I'm trying to put you through. All I know is that, for the first time in what feels like years, I have something to smile about, laugh about, feel carefree, without any drama. I'm not going to be sorry for falling- falling in love."

I was stunned. I didn't know what to say. It wasn't what I expected. I'd never heard someone admit it first. I was always the one to say it first.

"You what? You *can't*."

"If you want me to go, then I can, but you needed to know." Liam went to stand up but I reached out and grabbed his hand to stop him.

"Don't go." My voice was barely audible. "I fell for you too and I didn't think I could. Not so soon. But I still have this enormous amount of guilt."

"No one can help who they fall in love with. I didn't think I was going to end up here, with you. I really didn't. Now that we both know where we stand, what do we do? What do *you* want to do?"

"I don't like secrets. This almost feels like an affair but, for now, we keep it to ourselves. See if what we've got is real and then we decide how we're going to implode the news to everyone else, to *Laura*."

Liam's eyes flickered; it was easy to see that he was upset with Laura after what she'd done. I hadn't even had a chance to speak to her yet; it was almost like she was avoiding me.

"Are you okay with that?"

Liam's hand cupped my cheek, stroking my face with his thumb. "We'll do this any way you'd like. I like our little bubble. You don't know how much I wish we were still in Venice, staying there like we'd planned."

"Me too." I leaned forward, pressing my lips against his. I'd missed the taste of him. How it felt to be with him. Now that he was in front of me, there was no denying it; whatever happened between us, I had no choice but to accept it.

I was falling in love with my best friend's ex and one day I'd have to face the consequences.

It was time to dive in head first.

"How about you remind me exactly what Venice was like?" I whispered against his lips, feeling them curl up into a smile.

"*That* I can do," he replied, pulling me into his lap.

chapter twenty-three

My legs straddled Liam and I hooked my arms around his neck, pressing our heads together.

"Hi," I whispered. His hands slowly inched down my waist, cupping my ass comfortably.

"Bring back any memories yet?" he asked.

"Not just yet."

Liam kissed me and I moaned lightly at the feeling of his lips against mine, the tender touch sending shivers down my entire body.

The wine and pizza was long forgotten as Liam stood with me wrapped around his body and walked the short distance over to my bed. He threw me down, my body bouncing on the soft mattress. I giggled, leaning on my elbows to look up at him.

"Now, this seems a little familiar." I teased, smirking as I watched Liam take off his shirt and chucked it to the floor.

"Good because this next part is a little less familiar." He nudged my legs apart with his knee and lowered himself down, his lips hovering over mine. "I want to make love to you. Show you how much you mean to me."

I think I'd made love before. At least, I thought I had. But hearing the words leave Liam's mouth littered my arms with goosebumps, skipping a breath like my heart skipped a beat.

"Okay." It was the shittest response anyone could give. But how does someone react when they've never felt as important and special before?

Liam pushed up my flimsy night shirt, trailing his knuckles over my soft skin. My eyes fluttered shut and I let myself believe we were still in Venice. He pulled my shirt off and then started to work on my bottoms, tugging them down to my ankles first, then letting them fall onto the floor. I was almost bare in front of him, only the soft lace of my red bra left.

He kissed the inside of my thigh, trailing his lips all the way up to the warmth of my pussy. His tongue licked my parting and I reached out for my bed sheets, hissing in pleasure. Every touch was electrifying. Liam carried on moving up my body, caressing each inch of my skin with his lips, leaving burning marks everywhere he touched, until he reached my lips again.

I pulled him closer, stretching our kiss out because I never wanted to lose the feeling of what it was like to be alive with him.

Liam reached underneath me, toying with my bra clasp. As each hook came undone, I felt relief. I pushed down my straps and threw it to the side. Liam's fingers brushed over my nipples, then he lightly pinched them, causing me to gasp.

"That's my girl," he mumbled, peppering kisses down my jaw. I moved my hand, finding his hardened cock in his trackie bottoms that was dying to be released. My attempts to tug them down were failures. In the end, Liam pulled away from kissing me and took them off himself, leaving us both bare.

"Show me how much I mean to you." I intertwined our fingers.

Liam lifted my hand to his lips, placing a small kiss, then letting go.

"Move up a little," he asked and I shuffled up further so my head was on the pillow. Liam knelt on the bed and lowered himself towards my pussy again. His hands curled around my hips, holding me softly.

His lips found my clit, softly suckling on the sensitive hood. I whimpered, losing myself in us. There was no urgency; he took his time with his face buried between my legs. The only sounds in the room were the wetness of me and his lips enjoying eating me out.

His tongue moved lower down, his tongue pushing inside of me, his nose pressed against my clit. The curl of his tongue parted my lips and the volume of my moans filled the room. Only, they were short lived as he moved back towards my clit, gently flicking his tongue, before lightly grazing it with his teeth.

I lifted my hand to finger his loose curls, toying with them as each nerve inside of my body ignited the longer his mouth pleasured me.

"Oh god, Liam," I cried out.

His only response was to bury his face into my pussy further. Yet, his pace never changed; he took his time making sure he admired every inch of me.

I was tip-toeing on the edge of coming; how could I not with Liam eating me out? He was awful; instead, he was edging me. Doing exactly what I'd ask of him, showing me how much I meant to him. That time was only a concept with us and it didn't matter if we were in Venice or at home in the UK: we worked.

Liam came up to breathe, the wetness glimmering on his upper lip and chin. Using the back of his hand to wipe it away he bent down again only to kiss me this time, his hand massaging my breast as he used the other to force me to sit up with my legs either side of his hips. Without breaking our kiss, Liam pulled me closer. Once his hard cock teased my wet hole, he sheathed me on it, causing me to gasp.

I began to circle my hips, wanting to feel every inch of Liam that I could. He held me closer, guiding me with his hands on my ass. I used one of my own hands to balance myself, leaning back to find a better angle, and then pulled Liam closer by the neck so our lips were connected as I thrusted my wet pussy onto him. Even Liam was starting to feel dazed as I came down deeper onto his cock. A quiet deep moan escaped his lips.

"Esme. Fuck, that's it, gorgeous." His words were breathless.

I'd never felt as connected to someone as I did with Liam at that moment. My healing heart cracked again, thinking about how I could lose him in the future. I hadn't even realised that my eyes began to weep. Liam withdrew concerned, forcing me to stop my movements.

"Are you okay?" His brows furrowed.

"I'm okay. I just... I never want to lose you."

"Venice will sink before I stop loving you." He had all but said the three little words, like they were on the edge of his tongue, and I wondered if he was just as afraid of this new exciting love as I was."

"Do you promise?"

"On every star in the sky." He pushed deeper inside of me and I gasped.

Liam lay me down on my bed and took control. Each thrust was deep and slow, like nothing I'd ever imagined. The bed frame rocked, making a creaking to the rhythm of his thrusts and my constant moans. My fingers found my nipples, circling them lightly to feel the pleasure my body was craving. My head was fuzzy, light as I glided high and higher, closer to the edge.

Liam tucked his head into my neck, kissing the side of my neck. Over his shoulder, I could see the perkiness of his ass as he thrusted into me, along with the lines of his back muscles.

"Liam,." I cried out as he angled himself to hit the sweet spot inside of me. He knew exactly what he needed to do to take me over the edge. I was so close, grasping onto the pressure building in my core.

"I need to feel you," he groaned. "I want you to see stars and then I want to come inside of you. Make you mine forever, Esme."

"I'm yours already," I whispered, pressing my lips against his shoulder.

One of Liam's hands reached down for my clit, rubbing delicate and slow circles. Then, just as he thrusted himself deep inside of me again, he pinched lightly. It was just enough to make me see stars, just like he wanted.

My body withered and my lips parted as I moaned and called out his name. I dug my fingers into the duvet as I arched back, chasing the high, and I never wanted it to end. My pussy tightened around Liam's cock and he groaned, releasing inside of me. Closing my eyes, I felt Liam empty himself inside of me.

He lifted his head, breathless, slowly pulling out of me. Only, I was surprised when I wasn't greeted by a kiss. His head disappeared between my legs again and I gasped, reaching for his curls.

"Liam," I begged as he grazed my swollen clit. It didn't stop him from burning his tongue inside of me again. There wasn't a chance to be stunned by his actions; the high came back to me. My moans became louder, filling every corner of the room.

His lips wrapped around my sore clit and I screamed, coming all over again as my eyes rolled into the back of my head. My entire body went limp from pleasure.

Liam came up for air and rolled onto the bed beside me. I managed to lazily turn my head to look at him.

"Tell me again," I whispered.

Liam smiled, reaching out to stroke my hip. "Tell you what?"

"You know what. That you love me. Properly this time, so I know it's real."

"I love you, Esme. I'm not going anywhere."

"I love you too."

Even after Venice sinks.

chapter twenty-four

I'd come to the conclusion that I must have fallen out of love a long time ago to be able to fall as hard as I had for Liam after finding the brunette beauty in Rob's bed. What had broken my heart that day was the loss of security, familiarity.

I refused to live like that anymore, not after waking up with such a glow. Everything felt different. The sun shining through my windows was brighter. The smell of toast was stronger. My sheets were warmer as I rolled over, panic quickly set in as I noticed they were empty. Then I realised why I could smell it. Liam was standing, half naked, in my kitchen, spreading butter with two steaming mugs next to him.

I sat up in bed and Liam turned to look at me with a smile on his face.

"Morning, gorgeous."

"Mornin'," I croaked.

"You didn't have a lot in. I planned on making you a fancy breakfast but there was nothing to use."

"Yeah, I still haven't managed to go shopping yet."

Liam walked towards me with one of my mugs and a plate of toast in his hand, placing them on the bedside next to me.

"Thank you." From the second I took a bite, I was ravenous, remembering that we hadn't even eaten the night before.

"We didn't have the pizza," I said as Liam pinched half a piece from my plate. I looked over at the coffee table to find everything had been packed away.

"Don't worry, I found some plastic boxes and put them in your fridge for later. I was thinking maybe I should cook for us soon. What's the point of dating a chef if you don't use him?"

My cheeks burned red as Liam pecked my lips. Hearing the word 'dating' coming from Liam's mouth made my heart thump. I was as happy as we were in Venice, happier, even. I was on cloud nine and nothing could bring me down.

"Are we really going to do this?"

"Only if you want to."

"I do but can we stay in our Venice bubble a little bit longer, please? I'm not sure how I'm going to explain myself."

"You don't have to explain yourself to anyone. But, if you want to keep this between us for now, I really don't mind."

"Thank you. Have you got work today?" I asked, picking up my tea for a sip.

"Yeah, I start in a couple of hours but I've got time to stay with you." He leaned in for a kiss.

I tried not to smile as his lips touched mine but I couldn't help myself. "I'd like that, really like that," I whispered.

"Mmm, good, me too." Liam kissed me again.

Domestic bliss came to mind. I thought I had experienced it before, with Rob, but it didn't compare to the easy flow of being around Liam. We'd found our pacing in Venice; we knew how one another worked and we worked well together.

Though, time passed far too quickly for my liking and, before I knew it, I only had half an hour to get ready for my lunch shift. It was not enough time to look presentable; I ended up brushing my teeth while trying to put my shoes on. Liam tried to make himself useful, cleaning up the kitchen - not that he needed to and I kept telling him that. I clearly wasn't used to someone doing something nice for me, just because they could.

"Do you need a lift anywhere?" I asked while shoving on my coat and ripping my bag up off the floor.

Liam stood next to the door and shook his head. "No, I'm good. Just get to work safely and text me later." He kissed the top of my head and I blushed.

"Okay, let's go."

When we reached the top of the stairs, I took hold of Liam's hand and swung our intertwined fingers as we walked down the steps.

I didn't want to leave him when we got outside. I would have done anything in that moment to be back in Venice. To run away from the mundane ins and outs.

"Bye." I looked up at him.

Liam raised his brow at me. "No kiss?"

"I mean, yeah, I was saying bye." I rolled my eyes and leaned up to kiss him, wrapping my arms around his neck. Liam kissed me back, sweetly. There was no stopping the smile that graced my lips.

"Bye," he whispered. "I love you."

"I love you too. Go, before I'm late." I gave him a light shove.

"Okay, okay, I'm going. I'll call later." Liam held up his hands and stepped backwards, before turning around and walking down the street.

Only a few weeks ago, I was driving to work with what felt like my life in tatters and, now, I was singing along to She Moves in Her Own Way again. I pulled up in the work's car park, snatched my tatty tote bag from the passenger's seat and climbed out. There was nothing that could tear me down not anymore.

Only, my world stopped spinning when I saw Laura standing outside of the country club. The guilt began to drown me but I forced a smile on my face as I greeted her.

"Hey, Laura, what you doing here?" I asked. It was then I noticed the look on her face. She was furious, so red that I had the feeling that her blood was quite literally boiling. My heart dropped to my stomach.

"How could you?"

"What?" I croaked.

"You and Liam."

I almost threw up on the spot.

"Laura, please let me explain." I reached out for her and she shook her head, stepping back. It was exactly what I wanted to avoid, for my own selfish reasons. I didn't have the strength to hold it together.

My eyes began to water.

"There is nothing you could ever say that would make me forgive you for this. You're a backstabbing bitch."

I shook my head. "You don't get to say that." My lips began to tremble. "You didn't even tell me you'd broken up, he had to tell me in Venice... I know I've fucked up but you don't get to stand there and tell me I'm a bad person when you cheated on him and didn't even have the balls to tell me."

"That has got nothing to do with you. I knew it, I knew you weren't alone! You know, it didn't even surprise me when I saw his football mate in town and he told me."

"You saw the damage cheating does and you did it to Liam, who has always been the kindest and sweetest guy to you."

"Oh, just look at you," she shouted. "Wrapped around his little finger. You're nothing but a lying little bitch."

"Please, Laura. I know it breaks all levels of girl code but please listen to me."

"Not a fucking chance. You're dead to me." Laura shoved past me, hard enough that it nearly took me off my feet.

The tears were free flowing down my cheeks, ruining the only bit of makeup that was on my face.

I was in love but was it worth losing my best friend over? Taking one look at the door, I shook my head and turned away.

My legs were running back towards my car. There was no stopping the sound of my heart thumping in my ears. I fumbled with my keys, trying to unlock my car. Once I was safely inside of my bubble, I let myself cry, just like I had after finding Rob in bed with that girl.

And now I was questioning if being in love was worth losing one of my oldest friends.

chapter twenty-five

I barely made it halfway before I had to pull up the car and get out. The toast that I had eaten in the morning ended up on the side of the road. I felt like the shittest person that ever lived. I deserved what Laura had said to me; what kind of person goes after her best friend's ex and falls in love with him?

Hunched over, I wrenched again, nothing left in my stomach. My tears were starting to stick to my face, my legs trembling. I didn't know what to do, my head spinning in a thousand directions. The guilt that had been threatening to drown me finally took hold.

With shaky legs, I stepped back towards the driver's seat, holding onto the car door. I slipped back inside, slamming the door shut.

"I need to call work," I whispered, reaching for my bag to ring my boss. My hands were twitching as I waited for him to answer.

"Hello?"

"Hey, Danny." Luckily, I sounded shit enough to fake being ill. What was one more lie? "I was driving to work and I've just thrown up. I thought I was going to be fine but I've felt sick all morning."

"Right, fine. Just get some rest. I'll find a way to get you covered."

"Sorry, Danny," I croaked.

"See you later, Es. I hope you feel better soon."

I drove home slowly, knowing that I wasn't a hundred percent okay; I didn't want to risk a crash. All I felt was relief when I parked up outside my block of flats.

I sat there for a while, just thinking. I wasn't quite sure how much time passed when I finally reached for my bag. All I knew was that my mind had stopped spinning and had gone quiet, too quiet.

My entire body felt stiff, like I was an emotionless robot, as I made my way back upstairs, slotting the key into the door. The second I stepped in, I was greeted with the lingering smell of Liam's aftershave. Closing my eyes, I inhaled.

I had to find a way to fix the mess my life had become. There were two options: stay with Liam and keep being happy or let him go, ending up *un*happy. There was no guarantee that Laura would ever forgive me, even if I never spoke to Liam again.

After dropping my bag on the floor, I walked over to my bed, perching myself on the end, running my fingers over the sheets where Liam and I had slept the night before. The sick feeling was still there at the pit of my stomach but I'd be surprised if I could even throw up again.

"Distract yourself. What would your mom do?" I said to myself. Clean, that's what she would do. I kicked off my shoes and headed straight for my chest of drawers. Tipping every piece of clothing out onto my bed, I started to refold everything in colours.

As if I needed another reminder of how shit everything had been recently, I came across an old t-shirt that belonged to Rob. I scrunched it up without hesitation, throwing it across my flat while screaming.

Shaking with anger, I grabbed a bag from the kitchen and dumped it in there, then opened my cupboard to get rid of his favourite coffee and the mug with 'His' in swirly writing. Every little thing left of Rob was dumped into the bag until there was nothing left to bring him back into my life. It was junk, pointless junk, sitting at my front door while I cleaned the rest of my flat.

It must have taken me hours, my studio was starting to get dark. Before I knew it, I'd changed around the whole layout, leaving myself with sweat patches and bruised toes from struggling to move my furniture around on my own.

My peace ended as my phone rang in my bag where I'd left it. I walked over, my limbs aching from my scrubbing.

Liam calling...

'Answer' or 'reject' were my two options.

I rejected it.

What happened *didn't* stay in Venice and it was going to ruin our lives. No amount of happiness was worth the upset that it had caused. So, it had to stay in the past.

As I put away my phone, I noticed the bag of Rob's stuff again, sitting there and rotting. Even though I looked like a state, a crazed ex, I needed the bag of shit out of my life.

The waves of sickness tried to return once I got into the car with his stuff on the back seat but I refused to be sick again. I turned the radio up as loud as my rattling speakers could take it, screaming the lyrics to 'Just Like a Pill' by P!nk at top of my voice.

The drive to his mom's house was muscle memory. I'd done it a thousand times before, except then, I had *wanted* to be there.

My parking was askew, hanging half off the curb. I slammed the car shut, storming my way to the front door, pressing the bell, maybe a little too hard. And, when I didn't hear the chiming from inside, I rammed my hand against the wood, again and again. Waiting for someone to open the door, I didn't care if it was him or his mom. I just wanted Rob out of my life. He was the catalyst; if he hadn't been such a slime ball, then I would have never been to Venice, fallen in love with Liam.

I hated myself for loving him and then I hated myself for that too. I didn't want to regret feeling the way I did about Liam. Not when it had been the first time in years I had loved myself and my life.

It was Rob that finally opened the door, standing there in a towel as if he was the most gorgeous man alive. Which he wasn't. My doting goggles had been removed, that was for sure; the sight of his bare chest made me want to throw up all over again. I didn't even know what I was thinking; I used to believe he was God's gift and I was the luckiest girl in the world.

I laughed out loud, looking like a mad woman. Rob's brows furrowed.

"What are you doing here? And why the fuck are you laughing?"

"Cleaned out my flat. Found some shit that belonged to you." I dropped the black bin bag at the bottom of his bare feet.

"And?" He shrugged.

I shook my head. I'd been in love with a heartless asshole, thought I could change him, make him happy. There was no real chance of that; he didn't know happiness and he didn't know what love was either.

"One day your emptiness will bite you in the ass, Rob," I told him.

"Are you done?"

"You know, for someone who has been non-stop ringing for almost two weeks, you really do know how to put on a good act, trying to make out like you don't care about anything."

"I don't have time for this."

"Why? Is *she* coming around? Maybe I should wait, introduce myself, tell her what a scumbag you are."

"It's got nothing to do with you. So fuck off."

I laughed at him in disbelief and went to walk away. He wasn't going to have the last word. Never again. I turned back.

"I hope you do a better job at pleasing her anyway and she doesn't have to fake it like I did because, honestly Rob, it's not all that." I glanced down at his towel as a pair of headlights pulled up into the drive.

Looking over my shoulder, I noticed that it was his mom. She rushed to get out of the car as soon as she saw me.

"Don't worry, I'm not here to cause trouble. But, in case you didn't know and he's spun some ridiculous story, your son is a lying, cheating bastard and not as precious as you think."

"Mom, she's-" Rob tried to open his mouth from the door.

I enjoyed the look on her face; she was ashamed. My job here was done.

Rob didn't dare say anything to me as I walked away, listening to his mom telling him to get inside as I climbed into my car.

I turned the key and drove off. Liam had made me happy in Venice but I'd made myself happy putting Rob in his place.

All I had left to do was find a way to get Laura to forgive me and to forgive myself, if Liam and I had any chance of a future.

My phone rang again the moment that I parked up outside my flat. Liam was calling; he'd know that I'd finished my shift by now. The last thing I wanted him to do was start worrying about me avoiding him, not when we'd finally got somewhere with accepting our feelings for one another. I picked up my phone, answering the call.

"Hey." My voice was shaky.

"Are you okay?"

Lies had torn my last relationship apart; I had no choice but to be honest.

"Something happened today." I cleared my throat, sitting up in my chair. "When I got to work, Laura was there, waiting for me."

"What did she say?" The panic in his voice was hard to hide.

"She knows. About us. Said one of your friends let it slip."

"Are you okay?"

A small smile danced on my lips, as he proved all over again how much he cared about me. He wasn't just running away and thinking about himself.

"Shook up. I feel awful. I've lost my best friend. And I don't know how to fix it."

"It's going to take some time. Please don't let this shut you off from us."

"I won't. It won't. I can't blame myself for falling in love, I can't, not after everything. Would you mind if I had a little time on my own to sort my head out?"

"Esme-"

"I love you, Liam. I'm not saying I don't want you. Want us. I need one moment. I'm working through everything and how about I see you Friday? I'll cook us dinner? Or we can go out?"

"How about we cook together?" he suggested.

"I'd love that."

"Are you sure you're okay?"

"I'm okay, I promise. I'll text you in the morning. I won't just disappear."

"I love you."

"I love you too. I'll speak to you soon."

"Bye, gorgeous."

I hung up the phone, leaning my head back and closing my eyes. I exhaled, trying to calm my heartbeat and my trembling.

I'd sort my head out, make sure I was okay before anyone else. I let Rob go and maybe I needed to let Laura go too. I was sorry for going behind her back but I wouldn't be sorry for falling in love. Then, there was the fact that Laura hadn't even told me that she'd broken up with Liam.

Not even starting on the fact she had cheated on him, claiming that he was scum and deserved better. There was no difference between them

Tomorrow would be my fresh start.
Nothing was going to get me down.

chapter twenty-six

The best thing about my studio flat was the fact I'd managed to find one with a bath which was rare. I'd never been more thankful for it as I lay down, bubbles up to my chin and a glass of red wine in my hand.

I'd spent the day being me, after leaving Rob in my tail lights. I needed a moment to be myself. Every time I'd had an unhappy thought or something that made my stomach churn come to mind, I distracted myself. I'd read a book, watched *Harry Potter and the Chamber of Secrets* and baked some really awful cookies because I didn't have unsalted butter.

Just before I'd gotten into the bath, I explained to Zoe what had happened. Her protective nature jumped into overboard as she planned to hunt down Laura and 'give her a slap'.

Now that I was unwinding, I was starting to miss Liam. I wanted to reach for my phone, call him and tell him to come over, but I knew that it was best for me to have this day alone. Then, nothing would be able to ruin my dinner with him tomorrow night.

Once my glass was empty and my stomach was rumbling, I reluctantly drained the bat, dragging a fresh pair of PJs onto my body when I'd dried off. Then, I reached for my jacket.

I loved living in a small town where turning up in your PJs to grab a takeout wasn't strange in the slightest. Though, the last time I'd been down to my favourite Indian was over six months ago, on our last double date with Laura and Liam. It was an odd feeling, walking into the building. My eyes couldn't help but glance at the corner we'd had our date as I walked over to the bar.

One of the servers spotted me and walked over.

"Hey, could I order a takeout please?"

She pulled out their notepad with a smile. "Of course. What can we get you?"

"I'll have a chicken tikka masala with pilau rice please. Then a garlic naan and, hmm, four poppadoms with mint sauce?"

"Is that everything?"

"Yes, thank you so much."

She quickly typed up my order on the cash register. "That'll be eighteen pounds, seventy-five please."

"I'll pay by card please."

The server turned the machine round and I tapped my phone.

It was there I felt like my whole world fell apart again.

I heard his laugh.

I hadn't heard him laugh like that in years but there was no ounce of doubt in me that it was him.

I whipped my head around the room, trying to find him. My eyes landed on the back corner, where he was sitting. The person he was with had their back to me but I didn't need to see their face to know exactly who they were. The same curly brown waves I'd seen in the bed went down her back and she reached over the table to take his hand. It was his co-worker that had been in his bed that afternoon.

Aimee from work.

I was frozen, not quite sure what I was meant to do. I'd let him go, there was no point starting another argument. Then, there was the part of me that wanted to see who she was, just once. Maybe she was prettier than me, then perhaps I'd partially understand how he ended up in bed with her and why the hell he'd taken her to *my* favourite restaurant.

My wish was granted. I watched her turn around and my life felt like one big charade as I saw her face.

Every drop of blood in my body boiled as I studied the girl he had cheated on me with.

The girl I had been meters away from.

I could have saved myself a lot of agro if I'd waited to see who it was that day.

Because, sitting opposite my ex boyfriend, in the middle of my favourite restaurant, the same place we had been going to together since we were fifteen years old, was my best friend.

Laura.

It was strange what details you noticed when your life was falling apart. I'd seen her hair that day in his bed but no longer than an hour later it was off my radar. My brain didn't dare to make the connection that the same woman who held me while I cried had been screwing the man that I loved.

Thinking was out the window as I marched towards their table in my fluffy PJs and coat.

"How could I?!" I snapped, standing behind them. The couples surrounding us all turned to watch the show as Rob lifted his head to look me in the eye. Laura's shoulders went rigid; she didn't need to look at who it was. After all, we were 'the best of friends'. "And you had the guts to tell me that *I'm* a fucking bitch."

I'd never been a violent person but, in that moment, knowing that she refused to look at me, I saw red. My hand darted out to take a fist full of her hair, forcing her to stand up and look at me while she cried out. His hands reached to take mine from her head. I let go. I had what I wanted. Her to look me in the eye and probably spout some more bullshit.

"Ow, fuck you," she squealed.

"Well, what do you have to say for yourself?" I stepped closer, our noses almost touching.

"What do I need to say to you? You fucked my ex, I'll fuck yours," she snarled.

I started laughing. "Oh, pull the other one. I know it was you in his bed that day and then you have the fucking audacity to hold my hand while I bawl my eyes out. What kind of sick person does that?" Laura looked away as Rob stood up to save the day. "Stay out of this," I ordered him, then turned back to Laura. "Give me my flat key. Now."

I held out my hand as Laura reached for her bag and took it out; it still had the keychain of the two of us at prom in school. Not that our friendship had meant anything to her. She smashed it down into the palm of my hand.

"Now, if you're done, will you fuck off and go back to your sad little life?" Rob scoffed.

"Nah, no, you aren't spinning this on me when you were sleeping with my best friend for god knows how long." I returned my attention back to Laura. "How long?"

No answer.

"How. Long?"

It drew more attention from people around us and my time was running short before the manager would split us up.

Laura turned back to look me in the eye.

"A year. Alright? Three-hundred and sixty-five days. Is that what you wanted to hear?" She rolled her eyes and my desire to shove her head in her food was intense.

"Why?" I stumbled.

"You can't help who you fall in love with." She shrugged.

"And you called me a fucking bitch for going to Venice with Liam? I've been beating myself up for days because I fell for him and there you were, sneaking behind my back with my boyfriend."

"Oh, you love him, do you? Liam, so proper and perfect? Do you want to know something about your perfect, little prince? He *knew*."

"What?" I laughed.

"He knew that I was with Rob. Found out a month or so ago. So, while you thought he was healing your broken heart, he was trying to get into your pants for some payback."

Just when I thought nothing could break me again, my cracked heart shattered into a thousand pieces. I wanted to cry and I was sick of crying. It was all I ever did anymore. My chest hurt, the pain worse than anything I had felt when it came to Rob. I stopped thinking.

Next thing I knew, my hand was raised and headed straight for Laura's face. Rob rushed forward, acting like her knight in shining armour, holding her close to his chest as she sniffled in shock. I scoffed and walked away, before any of the servers could grab me. Spotting a carrier bag on the counter, I checked the order name. Seeing mine, I snatched it up. Not that I would even eat it now.

Most of the time, I could pull myself together enough to drive myself home but, as soon as I sat down and locked myself in, I screamed, smashing my hands on my wheel.

How could he have not told me? He had so many opportunities but decided to fuck me and make me fall in love with him.

Trembling, I dialled Zoe.

"Hey girlie, what you up to?"

"Zo. I'm at the curry house. Please. I-"

"Esme, what's wrong?" She was panicking. I made out rustling in the background, knowing that my real best friend was scrambling to shove her shoes on.

"I can't drive. Can you come please?"

"What's wrong?" she repeated herself.

"I know who Rob cheated on me with. It was... It was Laura."

"What. The. Fuck. I'm gonna be there in ten minutes, fifteen max. I'm ordering an Uber. I'll be right there, okay? Just hang in. I love you."

"Okay," I croaked.

I should have never gone to Venice.

It was the worst mistake of my life.

chapter twenty-seven

The tap on my window brought me out of my trance. Standing on the driver's side was my colourful best friend, her pink hair familiar to me as ever. I could see the pity in her eyes but I didn't have the energy to say anything. After opening the car door, I climbed out and silently walked over to the passenger's side, Zoe getting in beside me.

She didn't say anything as she drove my car back to the studio but she glanced at me when she could, examining my mood for a few seconds at a time. My head was pressed against the window and I watched the streetlights, counting them. Anything to not think about what Laura had said.

Only, sometimes I did, her words echoing continuously, and I could feel the tears creeping back. Every time, I swallowed and squeezed my eyes shut, begging them to go away.

Zoe turned off the car and I heard her sigh.

"Esme. Talk to me. We're home now."

Blinking, I turned my head to face her.

"It was her all along, Zo... Laura... She was the girl in Rob's bed; she was still there when you texted her and then she pretended. And, that's not even all of it." My voice cracked, tears threatening to spill.

"What else?" I could tell that she was ready to kick off.

"Liam, he knew. The whole time. He let me fall in love with him and he knew the whole time. He just wanted to get his own back and hurt Laura."

Zoe grabbed me, comforting me in her arms. I cried, knowing that I was at least safe in that moment.

"I'm gonna stay with you tonight," she whispered. "We'll eat the food you've got and put the world to rights. You're gonna be okay, I promise. If Rob, Laura or even Liam try to come anywhere near you, then they are gonna end up with one hell of a sore head." In an attempt to comfort me, Zoe rubbed my back; it was a rare occasion that my friend was so softly spoken. "Come on, let's get you inside."

I allowed Zoe to guide me back upstairs, draping myself against the wall as she unlocked the door, then ushered me. The smell of Liam was gone and I was grateful. There was no way I'd ever be able to forgive him for what he had done to me.

Zoe put the food in my kitchen as I walked over to my bed, climbing in and pulling my duvet up to my chin to pretend that the outside world didn't exist.

"Are you hungry?" Zoe asked.

I shook my head even though she couldn't see me.

"Okay, I'm worried about you. You scream and cry and rant. I don't like that you're shutting down on me."

Zoe laid down in the bed next to me so we were face-to-face. She pulled down the duvet a little so she could actually see me.

"I love him," I admitted. "And, all that time I was falling in love with him, he knew that Laura and Rob were in bed together."

"I know, you've been through enough. I can't believe he didn't tell you."

"He said that he was in love with me. Do you think it was real? Laura said it was only to hurt her."

"I don't know, Es. I wish I did." I hated seeing the pity in her eyes. I didn't want it.

Before I could open my mouth again, my phone rang from the floor where I'd dumped my coat. Zoe rolled over and grabbed it from my pocket, her face turning red with anger.

"It's Liam." She passed it to me. "Its up to you, I'll tell him to fuck off if you want."

My head was pounding as I looked down at the caller ID, my finger hovering over the answer button, ready to give him a piece of my mind. Instead, I rejected the call and threw it down to the end of the bed.

"Maybe you need to hear him out?" she questioned.

"So I can forgive pathetic excuses as to why he hurt me? I think not. I'm done with men that think they can do that to me."

"I know, babe. I know." She brushed my hair out of the way. "Look, can you try and eat something for me?"

"Zo-"

"We can cuddle up on the sofa. Please."

"I'm staying in bed but you can spin the TV around."

"Okay. Good." Zo sat up in bed with a smug look on her face, proud of her small accomplishment. "I'll move the TV and then warm up the food."

I forced a smile onto my face and I knew that she appreciated it, even if she didn't believe it was real.

While I dragged myself to sit up in bed, Zoe dragged the TV over towards me, then dished up the curry and put it in the microwave. I pulled my duvet closer to me again, needing the comfort of warm fabric against me, as my phone rang. I watched it, refusing to take my eyes off it. Zoe kept glancing at me, seeing if I would answer it.

Then, it stopped and there was silence again.

"Next time he calls, I'll answer," she spoke.

"It's fine, he'll get the picture." I shrugged, then looked away.

Only, that wasn't the case at all. I couldn't even enjoy a mouthful of rice before there was a knock at the door.

Zoe and I looked at one another.

There were a few options to who it was: Laura, Liam or maybe a neighbor, who wanted some sugar.

Another knock.

"I'll get it. If it's him, I'll tell him where to go."

I reached out to stop her but no words came out of my mouth as she began crossing the room to my front door. She put the chain on, before opening it a crack.

"What do you want?" she snipped.

"Please let me see her."

Liam.

I pushed my food to the side and got out of bed, ready to run into the bathroom and hide.

"She doesn't want to see you." Zoe shook her head.

"I need to explain. Please. *Please*. I never wanted to hurt her. I never wanted her to know; it would break her heart... it *has*. Please, I love her."

His begging made my head throb.

But courage came from somewhere, maybe from how life had been beating me lately, and I pulled Zoe away.

"Esme-"

"It's okay." My voice, however, wasn't as brave as my brain. It was rough and broken from all the crying.

I stepped into view through the crack of the door. I hated seeing him there; he looked good, his curls wild and unruly. Even dressed in a pair of tartan PJ bottoms and white t-shirt. Yet, here I was, a mess, all because of him. Just when I thought I was going to be happy again, it had been ripped from me.

"Esme, Es, please let me in and I can explain." Liam's eyes were glazed over but they weren't as red raw as my own.

"Did she call you? I bet she did. I thought she would never hurt *me*, I was her *best friend*. But, here we are, though she never hurt me as much as you did."

"Esme, I didn't want to hurt you. It's why I never told you. I couldn't break you like that. I should have said it that night at the bus stop but how could I when you were so upset? The fact you weren't even aware that we'd broken up told me everything I needed to know. I just wanted to make you happy again."

"Well you've managed to do just the opposite. We're done."

"I love you." Liam's eyes started to water.

I love you too.

I shook my head, refusing to feel guilty for his tears when he had caused so many of mine.

"Then you should have told me the truth." I managed to find the strength to close the door. Only, that was the last of it used up because I dropped to the floor, grateful that he could no longer see me.

Zoe wasn't too far away. She wrapped me in her arms, just like before, and I cried harder.

I loved him so much and I never expected to have to lose another person so soon. I was beginning to think that I was cursed.

Two guys in a matter of weeks?

Must have been a record.

chapter twenty-eight

Turns out, when you bed rot for forty-eight hours, your best friend drags you from your pit. That's how long it had been since I'd found out that Liam knew Laura was sleeping with Rob.

Liam hurting me was worse than what Rob had done. I didn't even stay in bed that long after I found out about Rob cheating. My armpits smelled, my hair was greasy and I'm pretty sure I had curry down my PJ top.

Zoe had her arms folded, staring down at me. I thought that, if I closed my eyes, she would disappear. Instead, that's how you get a pillow thrown at your head.

"Ow," I mumbled.

"I'll give you something to complain about in a minute. Come on, you need to shower. It'll make you feel better."

"Later," Grumbling, I rolled over to bury my face in my pillow.

"No, now. We're going out. You can't hide away forever. You need a drink and to let your hair down. Boys are not worth it."

"I don't wanna."

"Esme. Please. I'm worried."

I huffed against my pillow.

"I'll even pay for everything."

Getting drunk seemed a little more tempting when it wasn't my bank card getting battered.

I turned my head to look at her slightly. My remaining best friend looked terrifying, as if the next thing to be thrown at me would be a glass of water or something that would hurt.

"Where?" I asked.

"Well, I was thinking that we hit up the new cocktail bar in town, the one that's a coffee bar in the day. It's small; we can sit in the corner or under the pretty fairy lights."

"Cocktail bar means I have to dress up."

"You know I don't offer this lightly but, if you get your ass up and in the shower, I will blow dry and straighten your hair."

I couldn't help but laugh a little; Zoe hated helping out with other people's hair.

I pulled myself up, shuffling to the edge and forcing myself to stand up. The only times I'd left my bed recently were to pee and I wanted nothing more than to just climb back under my covers. Instead, I stumbled forward, knowing that Zoe would resort to desperate measures if I didn't move.

Zoe was right: I *did* feel better. Underneath the shower stream, I was able to wash almost everything away. Still felt like shit coming out of it, though.

Walking back out into the room, I saw Zoe had made my bed and got out my hairdryer and straighteners, ready near the edge of my matteress.

"Sit." She pointed with my hairbrush and I sat down obediently on the floor, my towel tucked around me. Zoe took the other one I'd wrapped around my hair from the top of my head and gently started to brush it through.

I found myself staring at the wall the entire time, wishing that I was feeling something. But everything became numbing and tiring. The last thing I wanted to do was go out. But I didn't complain when the heat hurt my head; I stayed quiet and let Zoe do her thing.

Once my hair had been dried and straightened, I hated to admit that I almost felt human again.

"Can you pick your own clothes?" Zoe asked.

"Yes, I can pick my own clothes." I rolled my eyes and headed towards my dresser, rummaging and trying to find something comfy to get away with. Only, instead, I pulled out the black dress with the metallic straps that I'd worn in Venice. It made my blood run cold.

"That looks cute. Why don't you wear that?" Zoe spoke.

"No, I've gone off it," I lied, shoving it back into my drawer again, looking for something else. I took out a white corset and baggy pair of black jeans. "This'll do."

Zoe looked at me but she didn't say anything.

The moment we were ready and I stepped outside, I wanted to run back in but Zoe held my hand the whole way down the stairs, as if she was too afraid I was going to run away.

While we were in the taxi, Zoe tried to make some conversation with me but I was too busy being lost in my thoughts.

I was beyond grateful for having her in my life. It was rare that your work friend would become one of the closest people in your life. And that she would end up as your *only* friend because your eldest one cared more about stealing your boyfriend and lying to you about it.

I wasn't stupid, going on holiday with Liam was wrong, but, considering what she had done, it was nothing. There was no need for her to break me any further than she had. I wondered how little she cared about me if she could do that after knowing each other almost all of our lives.

The taxi pulled up on the corner of the curb and Zoe pulled a ten pound note from her bag to give to the driver. I slid the door open and stepped out onto the street. The sun was starting to set which meant there was chill in the air and I hadn't brought a jacket. I wrapped my arms around myself as Zoe climbed out, slamming the door shut.

"Smile." She pointed at me.

I forced a sarcastic grin onto my face and Zoe rolled her eyes, slinging her arm over my shoulder.

"Come on you!" She laughed as we walked towards the door of the rustic cocktail bar.

It truly did transform at night. It looked nothing like the coffee shop. Instead, there were fairy lights decorating the bare brick walls, with a live band playing on the small stage in the corner. Most of the people drinking were gathered around listening to the music, others were scattered at the back, taking a seat at the high tables and stools.

"What do you want to drink?" Zoe asked.

I took a deep breath, knowing that I needed to make the most of the night, even if it was to just make Zoe feel like she was helping.

"I say let's make our way through the entire menu and see who throws up first." I smirked.

"That's my girl."

The first drink on the menu was a strawberry martini, followed by a tequila sunrise. There was no going back as soon as we had mixed spirits.

Once we were on the third round, I started to feel the buzz; that was enough to help me forget. Finally feeling a little more myself for the moment, I danced, swaying my hips to the sound of the music.

Only, for a split second, I remembered the last time I had done that. It was with Liam, that night in Venice, when we drank cocktails all night and slept together for the first time. The twinge in my heart nearly knocked me out. I gripped onto the table, staring down at my drink, before picking it up and necking it.

"Wow, girlie, slow down." Zoe laughed.

Ignoring her comment, an overwhelming heat flush coursed through my body. "I need some air. Coming?"

"Yeah, I could do with a vape." Zoe picked up her drink and bag.

I led the way, holding my hand out behind me for Zoe as we navigated the crowd and walked out into the beer garden which was decorated with large light bulbs hanging from the fencing. The heaters were on full blast, even though it was almost the height of summer. Little groups gathered under them but Zoe and I stood tucked away in the corner as she pulled out her little disposable vape. My friend quit a long time ago but something about drinking made her still smoke socially.

"Are you feeling any better?" she asked.

"A little. I'm trying, at least." I shrugged, resting my head against the fence.

"You had a hard knock. You'll get back up again." She smiled at me, in an attempt to make me feel better.

There must have been something about me that was easy to shock, that or I had really fucking terrible luck. I could hear a laugh, one that made my skin crawl, urging me to look over Zoe's shoulder. It was as though the crowd was parting just so that I could see her.

There, standing in the back corner, was Laura, laughing.

I couldn't take my eyes off her. I felt sick to my stomach, the way her brunette hair flowed. All I could picture was her laying in that bed, hoping I didn't realise it was her.

"Earth to Esme." Zoe waved her hand in my face.

"Hmm?" I blinked, looking at her.

"What's up with you?" She furrowed her brows and then looked over her shoulder. Almost instantly, she spotted Laura standing with her work friends under the gazebo. "Hell fucking no is she ruining our night."

My attempt to grab her wrist as she stormed off was a failure. Zoe was heading straight for her and Laura didn't even see her coming. Not until Zoe had smacked her around the face and nearly had her crumbling on the floor. Everyone in the beer garden had turned to look at the comotion.

I stood there, shocked that Zoe had actually clocked her around the face.

"What the fuck?" I heard Laura growl, beginning to step towards them.

"That is for being a spineless, little bitch." Zoe pointed her finger. "I'm not even finished with you yet."

"How about you back off?" One of Laura's work colleagues stepped in; I recognised her from a work event I'd gone to with Laura. And I knew Laura didn't even like her that much; she'd spent the whole day complaining about the woman.

"Has she told you all about her new boyfriend?" Zoe scoffed. "The way she literally fucked him while he was still with his girlfriend?"

I grabbed her shoulder.

"Zo, let's go." I pulled her back.

It brought Laura's attention onto me as she rolled her eyes.

"Well, look, she came out of her pit." Laura sniggered.

I bit my lip. She wasn't going to win ever again. She'd taken everything from me and I couldn't believe I'd spent a second feeling guilty about Liam knowing what I know now, seeing who my best friend really was.

"Do I need to shut your mouth for you?" Zoe snapped.

"Zo. It's not worth it. Rob will only cheat on her as well. He gets bored and makes you feel worthless, then finds his new model. She'll know how it feels before long."

I managed to drag her away and, looking over my shoulder, I watched Laura stand there, just as surprised as I had felt.

She was poison and I was glad to be rid of her. It was time to move on with my life. Live for myself and surround myself with the people who made me happy.

chapter twenty-nine

I woke up to Zoe's elbow smushed into my cheek. My best friend was a pain in the ass to share a bed with. I groaned, rolling over to give myself some space.

My head was hurting and I regretted every ounce of alcohol I had put into my body after we had seen Laura. There wasn't much I could remember about after either; the only thing still in my mind was the row of shots we had gotten when we went inside.

Not that I wanted to but I sat up and peeled my eyes open. I noticed there were three bags from McDonalds on the side which gave me a vague memory of forty chicken nuggets and too many fries.

I groaned and held my head, stumbling out of bed in nothing but my bra and pants. Unhooking my dressing gown from the bathroom door, I wrapped it around my body.

I yawned, heading over to the kitchen, picking out a cold chicken nugget from the box on the side. Weirdly, they always tasted better cold, at least to me. Then, I crossed the room, heading towards my sofa, where I spotted something poking through my letterbox. I frowned.

Whatever it was was covered in tissue paper, with a bow. I took it from the letterbox, confused, starting to tear at the paper as I sat down on my sofa.

Underneath the paper was a photo album which left me even more confused, until I opened it. There was a picture of the hotel and beneath was scrawly handwriting: 'Venice with Es'.

I started to flick through the pages. Most of them were just scenic moments but there, in the corners or edges, was an elbow or some blonde hair. In almost every photo, I was there but Liam had followed the rules and you could never tell they were photos of me.

Then on the last pages were the two pictures Liam had taken of me. The one from the gift shop with the stained glass shining on me and the other on the gondola ride. He'd lied; he never deleted the pictures at all.

I dragged my fingers over my smile, closing my eyes to remember how happy I was. Only, it made me feel worse. I was miserable... everything had turned to shit.

Curling up on the sofa, I spent the next hour flicking through the book. He must have spent ages putting everything together, choosing the best photos, because each one was perfectly aligned and taped in. Looking back and thinking about our trip made me want to reach for my phone, text him, talk to him. He'd still been trying to speak to me since I shut the door in his face and I'd ignored every attempt.

After seeing Laura, though, seeing her so happy with her life, I didn't want to stay so lost, not when she had been the cause of it and I'd not done a single thing wrong. Even if I had thought I had the entire time I was on the trip. I'd wasted all that time thinking I was a terrible person when, in reality, my so-called 'best friend' had been the one that had betrayed *me*.

Before I could make a decision on texting Liam, I noticed Zoe was sitting up in bed, watching me. I faked a smile, putting it to one side.

"I'm okay, I promise," I told her, before she could even ask.

"What was that?"

"A photo album. I think Liam posted it through the door. It was all the pictures from Venice."

"He seems to like you as much as you like him."

Part of me itched to correct her: *love*, not like. He loved me as much as I loved him. As he'd said, Venice would sink before we stopped loving each other. But that didn't change what he had done.

"He still lied."

"I know. He hurt you badly. I've never seen you like this and that's why I think it's so real. Maybe you need to talk."

"You've changed your tune. You were ready to kill him the other day."

"Well, that was until I just saw you smile for real without the help of alcohol."

I shrugged, pushing the album under a sofa cushion so that I didn't have to look at it.

"I need to wake up. I'm on the late afternoon shift and I can't go in hungover So, I'm going to shower," I spoke, changing the conversation.

"Yeah, me too. I'll order some breakfast and then head home. Is that okay?" she asked, picking up her phone.

"Yeah of course." I stood, walking towards my bathroom. "See you in a minute." Shutting the door behind me, I pushed my body against it sliding down, feeling sick for more than one reason.

When I finally got into the shower, I managed to wash my body, not bothering with an attempt to clean my hair. I didn't have the energy to stand up for longer. The energy I *did* have, I needed to save for work.

Soon after, I stepped out of the bathroom with my towel wrapped around me. Zoe had made the bed and was dressed in one of my tracksuits, scrolling on her phone.

"Did you order?" I asked, heading towards my clothes drawers.

"Mhmm, we have bacon, egg and hashbrown baguettes on the way, with caramel iced coffees," she replied.

My stomach churned a little at the thought of food.

"Do you know what you're gonna do yet?"

"Work, get my life together, one day at a time," I answered, finding some comfy clothes to do for the moment.

"And Liam?"

I paused for a second at his name. "There can't be a 'me and Liam'. He lied, hurt me. That's the end of of it."

And I would never let myself be hurt like that ever again.

chapter thirty

I took a deep breath, several deep breaths, as I sat in the car park at work. Last time I even tried to set foot in the place, I had Laura there waiting for me. Although I doubted that she would ever come near me again, something still stopped me from getting out of the car.

Every few seconds, I thought about calling my mom, getting a pep talk, but I always put the phone down again.

"Come on, Esme. Stop being such a baby," I muttered to myself, wrapping my hand around the door handle. If I let Laura and Rob ruin my job, then I really was screwed. Decided, I pushed the door open, finally getting out of the car.

I took the walk slowly across the car park, looking out for any surprises. When I made it to the entrance, I felt like I could finally breathe properly.

"See, no need to be a baby," I whispered as I headed into the building.

I went over to the bar and waved to Zoe, who was pouring a beer. She smiled, nodding at me as I beelined for the staff room to dump my things.

While I was there, I took a minute to myself, checking that I looked okay in the mirror. Not my best but decent enough that everyone would assume I just had a rough night's sleep and not that my best friend had broken my heart, taken my ex boyfriend and then ruined my new relationship with her ex. But who would even be able to guess that shit show, anyway?

I plastered a fake smile onto my face as I stepped out into the hallway and headed back towards the bar. Zoe caught me in the corner of her eye and excused herself from the country club members.

"Hey, you'll never guess what! Danny allowed a last minute private party in the function room."

"But we're about to get hit with the rush?" I huffed. Leave it to Danny to make a harder night even tougher.

"I know but I'm good here. So, do you think you can get it sorted?" she asked.

"How long have I got?"

"Maybe like half an hour."

"Great. Yeah, leave it with me." I turned around, calculating the best way to get it done quickly.

"Thanks, Es," she called.

Knowing that I was on a time crunch, I went straight into the store room and grabbed the first stack of table cloths I could find. With that sorted, I went towards the back of the building, to the private function room, which, in my opinion, cost way more to hire than it was even worth.

I was almost out of breath when I pushed open the door with my back, only to drop the pile of fabric as I saw what was going on inside of the room.

It wasn't as empty as I expected. Instead, it was lit with candles all the way around the room, different shapes and sizes giving off a warm glow. They led all of the way to the sliding door that went to the garden. The sun hadn't set just yet but it was growing dimmer by the minute. I assumed the candles would look even better then.

A silhouette stood by a table on the gazebo, stepping forward to reveal himself.

Liam was dressed in a smart white shirt and black trousers, holding a bunch of roses, his curls all perfectly coiled, along with a fresh shave.

My head told me that I needed to run away but my heart made me stand still and let him approach me.

"Hey, these are for you." He passed me the flowers and, with a trembling hand, I accepted them.

"How?" I croaked.

"Zoe. You were in the shower this morning, she answered my call."

That little fucker, I thought to myself.

"After she threatened to chop off my balls, she offered to help. To get you to at least hear me out."

"I don't need to hear you out. You *lied*, Liam." I sighed, shaking my head, refusing to allow myself to forgive and forget.

"Would you have told the truth?" he asked. "Would you have told someone who looked like their world had just ended? I'm a people person; I like to make them happy. I wanted to tell you so many times. And then, before I knew it, I'd fallen in love with you and it was done to me to make you happier than anyone had ever done before. I'm sorry for keeping it to myself... I know I should have told you but I just couldn't bring myself to make you hurt again, not when I'd finally got to see you smile, a real smile for the first time in years."

"Okay, okay." Knowing Liam, he probably could have gone on apologising forever.

"Please, Esme. Let me show you how much I love you. How *sorry* I am."

I brought the roses up to my nose to smell them, before I gave a shy nod.

"You have an hour."

"Zoe got your shift covered."

"You still only have an hour."

Liam sighed and held out his hand. Reluctantly, I took it. The moment our fingers touched, I realised how much I'd missed him being around. It was crazy to think how my life was so empty without him, almost void of joy. Joy that I didn't even think I'd feel again.

He led us outside to a table that had been set up with wine and candles, two silver domes placed either side. Liam pulled out my chair for me to sit down, then pushed my seat back in again once I was comfortable.

"Thank you."

"So, dinner might be a little bit cold. You came in a little later than I expected."

"Sorry about that. It took me a moment to get out of the car. Last time I was at work, I had Laura ready to tear me apart for being anywhere near you. That was before I knew what she had done."

Liam lifted the silver dome off in front of me, revealing a bowl of carbonara with garlic bread placed on the side of the bowl.

I couldn't stop the smile on my face as I put down my roses to give the food my attention. Liam sat down opposite me and took the lid off his own food. Afterwards, he picked up the bottle of pre-opened red wine and started to pour us both a glass.

"Thanks." I picked it up and took a large gulp, not ladylike in the slightest.

"Anything for you," Liam spoke and I knew now that he meant it.

No one had ever done anything so romantic for me in my entire life, not even my year one boyfriend who gave me half of his orange at snack time once. And definitely not Rob. His idea of romance was ordering a kebab and watching some really awful action films.

I picked up my fork, twirling it around my bowl to get a taste. It tasted amazing and I'd almost forgotten that Liam was a chef. All we'd eaten together was pasta and pizza made by others.

"So, did you make this?" I broke the silence.

"Yeah, then Zoe asked your head chef if I could warm everything up in the kitchen."

"I'm gonna kill her when I see her." I laughed, grabbing another mouthful.

"She only wants what's best for you."

"And what? That's *you*?" It came out a little harsher than I intended. It wasn't what I wanted to say and perhaps I was still holding onto some of my anger. It was almost like I needed to hear him say it, just to be sure he was the *one*.

"I've put you first since that night at the bus stop and I won't ever stop. I promise you."

"I'm sick and tired, Liam." I put my fork down with a sigh. "I can't take it anymore. I want to be happy with you but I'm scared."

"I know and there's nothing left that can upset you. Even if something does, I want to be there for you. Esme, I love you."

"And I love you."

"Please give me one more chance." Liam's voice cracked. "I'm so, so sorry." I could see tears forming in his eyes. Liam was hurting without me, just as much as I hurt without him.

"I know you are." I swallowed. There was no pushing it away anymore; I had to decide if I was going to stand my ground and move on without Liam or give it a chance, knowing in my heart how much I adored him. "I think maybe we can. We can try one last time. For real. No hiding and no secrets."

"Es, you won't regret it. I swear it. I just want you to be the happiest woman alive and I want to be the one to make you happy."

"It might take some time to build the trust back up."

"I'll do whatever it takes. I'll never risk your trust ever again; it's too important to me." Liam reached over the table, holding his hand out to me, and I took it gratefully.

"I know you won't."

"Here, I have something for you. I know it doesn't make up for what I did but I got this on the way home." He pulled a little blue box from his pocket and handed it to me.

I took off the lid to reveal the tennis bracelet with baby blue crystals that I had looked at the day we'd left for Venice. My lips parted in shock.

"I wasn't sure when I should give it to you but right now seems a better time than any other. I don't want us to ever forget our trip to Venice. Not when it gave us so much happiness and each other."

chapter thirty-one

Liam walked me to my door after I drove us back. I leant my head against the door, smiling.

"Well, I'm home safe and sound."

Dinner had been perfect. After we'd finished eating, Zoe had come in with dessert and a smug look on her face. Liam and I had talked a little more about what happened, telling me how he'd seen Laura outside of Rob's house, then confronted her about it. It gave us the opportunity to put what had happened to bed.

If we hadn't, there was no way that we would ever be able to move on and be happy.

"So you are." Liam tucked a piece of my blonde hair behind my ear. It amazed me how one slight touch made shivers run down my spine.

"Goodnight, Liam."

"Night, gorgeous." There was a split second where I thought that was it for the evening, leaving me disappointed.

Only, he didn't stop there. Liam took his chance to capture my lips against his. I hummed against him, wrapping my arms around his neck.

"Come inside," I whispered.

Liam nodded slightly and put his hand into my bag for my keys, opening the door for us. His lips never left mine, getting hungrier with every second. He kicked the door shut and pushed me against the wall, finally breaking our kiss.

"Tell me to stop, else I won't."

"Then no, I won't tell you to stop." I giggled.

Liam's fingers hooked inside my blouse, between the buttons. I gasped when he ripped it open, revealing my nude bra.

I raised my brow at him. "Really?"

"Hope you have more uniforms." He shrugged. "Any requests?"

"Hmmm, make me see stars." I smirked.

"*That* I can do." Liam cupped my face and pulled me in for a hard kiss, taking my breath away. As I shrugged off my shirt, Liam directed us towards the bed.

I bounced on the mattress when he pushed me down, making me giggle. Liam made light work of his fancy shirt and trousers, then brought his attention back to me. He pulled off my work trousers so I lay before him in mismatched underwear.

My boyfriend pulled down my underwear and pushed my thighs apart, pressing small, chaste kisses along my spine. The suspense of him reaching where I wanted him to be was killing me, until he finally licked a line up my pussy.

"Liam," I called out.

"Yes, gorgeous?"

"Why don't we make sure we're both getting a little pleasure?"

Liam lifted his head, curious.

"Are you suggesting what I think you are?"

"Would that be scandalous after you fucked me in our hotel window?"

Liam didn't need anymore convincing, laying down the bed. As he took off his boxers, I turned my body, straddling him so that my pussy was hovering over his face.

His cock was hard against his stomach and I wrapped my hand around it, slowly caressing it before placing my lips around the tip.

Liam gripped my ass, pulling me down so my pussy was flush against him. I moaned as his tongue flicked my clit, knowing the vibrations would make Liam's eyes roll.

I took more of his cock into my mouth and what I couldn't fit I used my hand for. The sensation of being pleasured while I sucked Liam made me wetter by the second. Before long, I could hear it with Liam's face buried in my pussy.

Liam's slow flicks soon ended as we got lost in the moment. He sped up, his tongue darting inside of me, lapping up every drop of wetness, then he swapped back to my clit. His fingers gripped my ass so tightly that the dull ache could have nearly made me come all over him.

With each second I lost composure, the blow job became sloppier. All that I could taste was Liam's pre-cum. I bobbed my head faster and faster, swiping my tongue underneath the head.

I glanced up at Liam's thighs, the muscles beginning to tighten as my wanton moans filled the room, making him start to whimper.

The knot in my stomach was about to explode. The thought of coming over Liam's face only made it worse. I didn't want to stop and tell him, not when I knew I had him so close. Sucking harder nearly made Liam lose his concentration as he moaned right against my clit. I swiped my tongue against his slit and Liam shivered.

Seconds later, my mouth was filled with hot cum and I swallowed every drop, my ears filled with Liam's grunts and moans. He stopped, taking a second to breathe, before pushing two of his fingers inside of me, his mouth giving all its attention to my clit.

Liam's cock had started to soften once I had cleaned off the remaining cum. Now that my mouth was empty, I was able to moan freely, as his fingers curled against the spot that brought me closer and closer.

I rocked my hips, begging for him. Liam smacked my ass and I cried out.

With one last thrust of his fingers, my entire body shook and I came over Liam's face, calling his name.

Once my legs stopped shaking from my high, I climbed off, my entire body going limp beside him. I placed my hand on my chest, trying to steady my breathing.

Liam lazily reached out to stroke my thigh.

"You okay?" he asked.

I hummed.

"You know I'm not done with you, don't you?"

I propped myself up to question him, only to see his other hand wrapped around his cock to harden it up for another round.

"What else have you got planned?" I tilted my head.

Instead of telling me, Liam decided to show me. Within seconds, he had moved me into the position he wanted me. I was bent over the bed, knees towards the end of it, with my back arched. Liam stood behind me, rubbing his cock down my wet pussy, sending a shiver down my spine.

Slowly Liam pushed himself inside of me which is all it took for him to be ready for the next round. He started gently thrusting into me, his hands placed on my hips, pulling me closer. The pace was almost relaxing, only it didn't last long. Liam soon sped up, his fingers digging into my hips.

"More," I begged. "Harder."

Liam granted my wish, his thrusts becoming harsher, wanting me to come over him again. My lips were parted, letting out every moan that my body produced; they seemed to will Liam on. He removed one of his hands from my hips and took my pony tail into his grip, yanking my hair.

The twinge of pain from my scalp had me tightening around him. Liam hissed in pleasure, his other hand massaging my ass, before he smacked his hand against it. My whole body shook as I came again.

Liam followed soon after. His cock twitched inside of me. There wasn't enough cum to fill me like he had before but Liam still enjoyed his orgasm, rutting out inside of me.

A sensitive moan left his lips as he pulled out and I rolled over, in bliss.

What surprised me was when three fingers pushed inside of me. I jolted up and grabbed Liam's arm.

"Liam!" I whined.

"I don't think you're seeing stars just yet."

His fingers curled each time they thrust inside of me.

"I can't."

"You can. One more for me. You're so tight, gorgeous, I don't think it's going to take long."

The pressure inside of me was different. I'd never felt anything like it before. Almost like-

"Liam, stop, please. I think... I need to go to the toilet." I would have thought that Liam would have stopped but his fingers only quickened as his eyes lit up.

"Yeah? Cause I don't think that's it. Trust building exercise. Relax for me."

I swallowed, letting go of his arm, trying to do as he asked. The pressure was stronger every time his fingers pressed against that one spot. The pleasure was overwhelming, I couldn't even speak anymore. All I could do was look Liam in the eye.

"You going to come for me, gorgeous?"

I nodded, the ability to form words gone.

"Scream for me when you do."

I nodded again.

Seconds later, I screamed as I came. Liam quickly pulled out his fingers and rubbed them frantically against my clit as I drenched my thighs, bed sheets and Liam's hand.

I collapsed against my mattress, eyes rolling into the back of my head, as my heart thumped in my ears. It took me a minute to regain my brain power and I dragged myself up to see Liam wiping his hand on my trousers, with a smirk on his face.

"Shit, my sheets." I jumped up and turned to see a huge wet patch where I'd squirted.

"Do you have spare?" he asked.

"Yeah, I'll get them." I went to find them but stumbled.

Liam caught me, scooping me into his arms. "No, you're gonna go have a bath while I clean up."

"I've never came like that before," I said, stroking his cheek.

"And it's not going to be the last. I need to see that every day of my life."

"You're so smug right now, aren't you?" I rolled my eyes, lazily, my body not having the strength to do much else. And god did I love that.

"Yes. Yes I am." And he carried me into the bathroom.

chapter thirty-two

Waking up the next morning was bliss on another level. My brain was getting whiplash from all the mental ups and downs since I had got back from Venice. I tried to concentrate on the fact that I was happily wrapped in his arms and nothing would stop me from being on cloud nine. I snuggled closer to him and closed my eyes again.

"I know you're awake," Liam mumbled.

"Wasn't trying to hide it. Just wanted to stay here a second longer, before we have to face the world," I whispered.

"Or we could just stay here today, pretend we're in our Venice bubble."

I rolled over in his arms, stroking away the free falling curls from his face. He opened his eyes and I smiled.

"We can't pretend forever."

"Worth a try but I think we could, at least for breakfast. Have you been shopping yet?"

"Zoe and I did an online order the other day."

"I was thinking pancakes?"

"That sounds perfect."

Liam kissed me and moved his arms to get up.

I propped myself up on my elbows, enjoying the view of his naked ass walking away from me. He went to pick up his trousers.

"Oh no you don't. This bed is perfectly positioned to watch you in the kitchen, I've always fancied myself a chef in the buff."

Liam looked over his shoulder and smirked at me, letting his trousers drop back on the floor.

"Do I at least get an apron?" he asked.

"You wish."

Liam chuckled and headed towards my small kitchen.

My eyes never left the gorgeous sight in my kitchen as he began to cook for me. A few giggles left my mouth when his equipment swayed while he mixed the pancake batter.

"If you keep laughing, I'll put some clothes on," he called over his shoulder.

"Hmmm, you still have some making up to do so I wouldn't, if I were you."

Liam flipped the pancakes and went searching for a plate, dishing them up, and adding some strawberries he'd found in the fridge.

"Golden syrup is in the far cupboard," I called.

"Of course, m'lady." Liam grabbed the bottle and then headed towards me.

He placed the plate in front of me and tugged down the duvet that was covering my boobs.

"Hey!"

"You get a show, then I get a show." His thumb grazed over my nipple, making me shiver.

"Hmm, fine." I rolled my eyes, picking up my fork, to take a mouthful.

Soon as the bite hit my taste buds, it melted in my mouth. I was in heaven.

"Good?"

"The most amazing pancake I've ever tasted," I answered. I couldn't stop smiling, questioning if this was what real love was like.

Liam sat on the edge of the bed, stealing bits now and then. There were no arguments, no treading on eggshells in case I said something wrong. It was real happiness.

I never wanted to let it go.

"Crazy thought," I said, putting down my fork. "You know how we talked about staying in Venice?"

"Yeah, still think we should have."

"So, what if we did? Make that our goal, find a little bar?" Liam didn't answer. I shook my head, regretting even suggesting it in the first place. "It's crazy, I know."

"Not at all because that's exactly what we're gonna do. We're gonna plan another trip, save up and, before you know it, in a couple of years, we are going to be back exactly where I fell in love with you. "

"I know what makes me happy now and that's you and Venice. That's all I need."

"You really don't need to try and convince me. I'm on board."

"Really?"

"Really."

I squealed and wrapped my arms around him, almost knocking over my breakfast.

"I love you," I whispered.

"I love you too and remember, Venice will sink before I stop." Liam kissed me which I was enjoying, until something crossed my mind.

"Shit, we're gonna have to learn Italian this time."

epilogue

I stood on Rialto bridge, exactly two years from the first time I set eyes on it. The sun was shining and I loved watching the tourists passing by.

We'd spent seven-hundred and thirty days saving every penny we could earn to get ourselves back in the city where we fell in love. Where we were going to live.

We'd found a bar that had been shut for a few years and Liam had made a deal with the owner that we would get it up and running again for a discount on the tiny flat that sat above it. It was one step closer to where we wanted to be.

I heard the click of the camera and whipped my head around to see Liam with his phone pointed at me. Raising my brow, I tried to snatch it out of his hand but he quickly lifted it up over his head, placing a kiss on my lips to distract me.

"Why are you always taking pictures of me?"

"Because you're beautiful." He slid his phone into his pocket and pulled me closer.

I was happily wrapped in his arms, despite our PDA that was probably putting everyone off. Liam shuffled on his feet and pulled away.

Only, what happened next had me stunned.

Liam dropped down on one knee and my eyes nearly popped out of my head. He opened the black, velvet box from his pocket. The ring was almost blinding with the sun, reflecting off the large diamond. A lot of people would say that it wasn't glam enough but the diamond and plain band was perfect for me.

I blinked twice, not quite believing what was happening.

Liam cleared his throat.

"Esme, my gorgeous girl, two years ago, we came to this city together and you changed my life, by complete surprise. I never want to spend a day without you. I want to be with you every second of our lives together. So, will you do me the honour of becoming my wife?"

I felt everyone on the bridge staring at us which made me feel really awkward, along with the shock.

I nodded slowly.

"You're gonna have to say the word," Liam teased. "Before my knees give way."

There were a few more moments of silence. I knew what I wanted to say but the words just wouldn't come out.

"Y-yes." I swallowed. "Yes, I'll marry you." My eyes teared up and Liam took the ring from the box, sliding it onto my finger, the ring glimmering under the sun. I held it up, not quite believing that I was engaged.

The crowd that had been watching us since Liam got down on one knee started to clap and I blushed red but Liam picked me up and spun me around.

"I'm going to be Mrs. Mcallister," I spoke, stunned, as he put me back down.

"Venice will sink before I stop loving you, Mrs. Mcallister."

"That's a long time," I told him as he put me down.

"Too right it is." Liam kissed me again, soft and tender, filled with love.

The main thing I've learnt in the last few years is that, sometimes, love doesn't last because it's making room for a greater love.

And I found mine.

acknowledgements

If it hadn't been for the fact my heart was broken a few years ago this book would have never had been written. Venice was exactly where I needed to be and heal, where I found myself again. So thank you to the city that made me whole.

A massive thank you to Faith and Emma for your support writing this and pushing me to make the story into a full length novel rather than a novella like I had originally planned. I wouldn't have been able to do this without you and I'm so grateful for our little group.

Another shout to Chelsea for being the one that actually booked our Venice trip, and her excitement for this book.

Last but not least my two girls in Australia, Al and T, who believe in me no matter what. And yes T before you say anything thank you for asking for me to write a friends to lovers book which ended up inspired What Happens in Venice.

about the author

Em Solstice is a romance author from the UK. As well as procrastinating writing fast-paced novels and novellas with a spicy twist, she enjoys snuggling her cat and drinking Starbucks... and waiting for her own love story to begin.

Printed in Great Britain
by Amazon